Stone Champion:

A Paranormal Protector Tale

Book 2 in the Heart of Steel series

DEMELZA CARLTON

This book was created with the assistance of a grant from the Western Australian Department of Local Government, Sport and Cultural Industries.

ONE

"Good morning, Auntie Callie!"

No one should be that cheerful first thing in the morning, Callie thought as she reached for a mug to make tea. Except…one look at little Rory's gap-toothed smile, and Callie couldn't stay grumpy.

"G'morning, princess," Callie said, grabbing the kettle.

That did it. "I am NOT a princess! I am a bounty hunter and I can bring you in warm or

I can bring you in cold!" Rory insisted.

"Does your mum know you've been watching the Mandalorian again?" Callie asked. So much for the parental controls on the TV. Rory seemed to be an expert at getting around them. Maybe she took after Octavia.

"Mummy watched it with me!"

Callie couldn't explain how, but she always seemed to know if someone was lying or telling the truth. And Rory was being absolutely honest, unlikely though it seemed.

Tacey having time to watch TV, even if it was a streaming service. Now that, there, said something was definitely wrong with the world.

"What did Mummy do this time?" Tacey strode into the kitchen, wearing her café blacks.

"Has the world gone back to normal again, so you're going to work?" Callie asked.

Tacey grinned. "Not quite, but on the morning news, they said the restrictions are easing soon. So we'll be able to open properly, and not just serve takeaway for the mornings. I'm going in to dust and put in some stock orders, so we'll actually have something to serve people." She patted Rory on the head. "C'mon, time for school."

"Yuck, Mummy! You said you'd get rid of it!" Rory screeched, pointing at a storage box that to anyone but a princess-hating six-year-old would be completely inoffensive.

"Oh, yeah. While we were cleaning up Rory's room yesterday, we found that. I think it's yours, Callie." Tacey tied on her sneakers.

"What is it?"

"It's a princess box! Princesses are boring!" Rory shouted.

"Put your shoes on, Rory." Tacey sighed. "It's a box of your old school books."

"Are you sure they're mine?" Callie poured hot water over the tea bag, inhaling the unearthly steam that rose up like it was the breath of life. It almost was.

"Yup. With CALLIOPE FERREIRA emblazoned on the front of them, it's hard to think they belong to anyone else." Tacey tucked her bag under her arm and picked up her keys. "See you tonight." Then both she and Rory were gone.

Leaving Callie alone with the Sleeping Beauty box and a fresh, steaming cup of tea.

She hefted the box onto the table and lifted the lid. Sure enough, Tacey was right – those shaky letters were hard to miss. She probably hadn't been much older than Rory, but unlike Rory, Callie had actually liked Disney princesses, hence Mum had liberally covered her books in every Disney movie imaginable. Callie could remember loving all of them. Except Cinderella and her fairy godmother, apparently, who she'd crossed out and scrawled, MAGIC DOES NOT EXIST over.

Callie sat back in her chair and sipped her tea.

Quite right, little Callie. Magic definitely does not exist, she told herself.

She lifted out the mutilated maths notebook, and several other Cinderella-covered books which had received the same treatment. Then she saw the cracked black leather and dropped the lot, hiding it from sight.

Sometimes, she thought she'd imagined it. That the book had just been part of her nightmares, a figment of her imagination amid the horrible memories. Yet here it was, real.

Magic does not exist, Callie told herself.

But books with magic spells in them…or spells that claimed to be magic, despite the non-existence of such things…yeah, those still existed. And this one held a power over her that had nothing to do with magic.

TWO

Grant knew one thing for certain: there was magic in the universe, and the universe used it to give him the most amazing adventures. Take today, for example.

Harlow slammed his empty cup on the table. "We are not robbing the mill and stealing a bride for Stan!"

Spoilsport. But that was Harlow, all over. It was hard to believe Grant was his brother. "Of course we are. Right, Stan?"

"Yes! We are proud and true Scots, and it is tradition!"

From the slur in his voice, it sounded like Stan had actually managed to get drunk on the watered down piss that passed for ale in the Swan River Colony. That would be a first.

"So, should we go in with guns blazing, like bushrangers?" Grant asked eagerly.

"We'd have to get guns first, and what if you actually shot someone? They'd send you to Van Diemen's Land for that, and no one comes back from that hell hole. No, we must use stealth, or not go at all," Wystan said.

Harlow turned on him. "You can't actually mean to support this lunacy?"

Wystan spread his hands wide. "Stan's in love, Harlow. Love cannot be reasoned with. That's why we need to help him. When you fall in love, you will understand. And we will help you, too."

Harlow scoffed. Grant was inclined to agree with him. Harlow was far too logical a man to ever fall in love with anyone. "If we do this, we'll wake up in chains tomorrow."

"Chains of matrimony. For Stan, at least. The sweetest, lightest chains a man ever wore," Wystan said dreamily.

Of course, he was not thinking of Stan or Carline, but of himself and his own dearly departed wife.

Grant only wished he'd have half Wystan's luck. Well, not losing his wife so early in the marriage, of course, but having someone he loved so desperately in the first place. A woman worth stealing. A woman who wanted him to steal her.

A woman who would come with him on any adventure, whose high spirits matched his own.

The sort of woman he had yet to see in this dreary Swan River Colony, which was mighty strange. A brand new colony, carving out land in the wilds on the other side of the world, begged for people with an adventurous spirit, but most of the women he'd seen here were…tired. Listless. No spirit to speak of, even if most of them weren't already married. Not that that would have stopped them if the lady were truly an adventurous spirit like himself…

Grant sighed. But he hadn't seen a single woman here who might stir his loins, let alone his spirit. Perhaps she was still aboard a ship, sailing to him right now. The universe was magical that way – there would be such a woman, as perfect for him as Stan's stolen bride would be for him. Grant was certain of it.

"So, it's settled, then. Tonight, we steal a bride for Stan, and he will be the first of us to wed. Then, we shall steal three more, when the time comes, until all of us are so happily situated, working our Murray River farms, that the devil himself will envy us." Grant lifted his cup of ale. "To a successful raid, like the days of old!"

Stan and Wystan lifted their cups, then looked expectantly at Harlow.

"Fine. To our last night as free men," Harlow said, and drank.

Grant couldn't help grinning. There was magic in the air tonight, he was certain of it.

THREE

Callie wasn't sure which was worse – university students, or the staff.

Usually, she'd say the students, but what with all the restrictions and lectures going online, the staff now outnumbered the students and seemed to be going more than a little stir-crazy in their offices alone.

But that was before the Fremantle zombie.

Yes, she had the largest collection of arcane

texts in the Southern Hemisphere. Yes, she knew more about medieval magic practices than the Spanish Inquisition. But she had never seen, let alone created, a zombie.

Unfortunately, the religious faculty members didn't believe her.

"The grave was desecrated less than a kilometre from your office!"

Christian's office was closer.

"No one has found the body!"

Maybe some kids had just dug six feet down for a prank. The hole was in a high school oval, for goodness' sake. Just because kids dug a hole in a century-old cemetery didn't mean they'd actually find a body.

"This office must be exorcised, so the zombie doesn't return."

Callie had offered to perform the exorcism herself – she was as fluent in Latin as any of the religious scholars – but the faculty head had insisted on the ritual being performed by a priest.

So Callie had gone up to see the second

hand bookseller she'd been meaning to visit, to pick up some rare books he'd bought as part of a deceased estate. She'd returned with three new books, which she piled on top of the cracked black leather one, in an office that now smelled strongly of frankincense.

Good thing she liked frankincense.

The rumours about the zombie had finally died down, when the internet discovered the Fremantle Moth Man.

After three people invaded her office without even knocking, demanding she tell them everything she knew about the Moth Man, Callie went to hide in the kitchen.

But they found her there, too.

"Good morning." Catena smiled, then opened her mouth as if to ask a question.

Oh goddess, not her, too! Catena worked in the library. She was usually such a sensible person.

Callie held up her hand. "Before you ask, let me stop you right there. No, I don't know anything about Moth Men. No, I didn't see it last night, and no, there are no historical accounts of anything even faintly resembling a Moth Man in any part of my archives, because a Moth Man is an urban myth, based on a hoax staged in some small town in America. There is no Moth Man, there never has been a Moth Man, and there never will be, because they do not exist!"

"What is a Moth Man, and why is everyone so interested in him, all of a sudden?" Catena asked, carefully.

Callie dared to breathe again. At least Catena still had sense. Callie waved her hand in dismissal. "It's a myth. The only reason everyone's talking about it is because someone dressed up in a bad Batman costume, filmed it, stuck in some special effects, and then posted the video online, where it's gone viral. Even the news websites have picked it up, because it's the second monster sighting in Fremantle in the last month, or at least that's what they're saying." She snorted. "As if zombies were real, either."

"There's a zombie in Fremantle?"

Catena had to be the only person in the world who didn't know. Callie warmed toward her even more.

"Of course there isn't. Not even a fake one – someone would have caught it on camera if there was. No, it was a prank pulled by some high school kids, I'm sure of it. Someone dug up an old grave at the first Fremantle cemetery, left some hand and foot prints in the soft soil around it. Like a zombie had risen or something, or at least that's the story the kids told, when they got to the police station. Something about a man shambling away. If you ask me, they probably disturbed some homeless man, sleeping in the bushes. Serves them right."

Catena backed away a little, her smile appearing forced.

Maybe Callie shouldn't have given her so much detail. But Catena hadn't had her office exorcised because of a hoax.

"Who'd have pegged Fremantle as Monster

Central? In the movies, it's usually some American small town, or the seedy parts of one of their cities. What next? Vampires? Demons? The Winchester brothers?" Now her smile looked real. *Supernatural* could do that to a girl.

Callie shook her head. "While I wouldn't say no to a visit from Sam and Dean, it's got to be a stunt. Monsters don't exist. At least, not the supernatural kind. Just people who do horrible things." She shrugged. "Watch the video for yourself. Search up the Fremantle Moth Man – you'll find it. See how fake it looks. We won't be hoping for a visit from the Winchesters or whatever their real life equivalent is any time soon."

She headed back to her office, but only long enough to pick up the four old books she wanted to scan. Then she spent the rest of the day in the rare books room at the library, carefully scanning each delicate page, and avoiding zombies, moth men and mad academics.

It was the best work day she'd had in weeks.

FOUR

Callie finished translating the third book from the deceased estate. The first two had been herbals, books that described how to make plant-based medicine for a variety of ailments. Some of them might have even worked. The third one, however, had been more of a witch hunting guide. How to recognise witches, and how to drive them off. While some of the things in the book could have been source material for a Monty Python movie, the rest was decidedly dark. As for witch bottles…Callie shuddered. Some knowledge really should stay lost.

But now she'd finished those three books, she really had no choice but to work on the cracked black leather one from the Sleeping Beauty box.

The one that didn't actually belong to her, because she'd stolen it, all those years ago.

Callie closed her eyes. She'd taken it to protect herself, because she'd believed it was necessary. Now…

"There's no such thing as magic," she said to herself as she clicked on the book's folder.

And…her phone rang.

She didn't even look at the number before she answered it, she was so relieved at the reprieve.

"Hello?"

"Callie! Did you see the news? They're lifting the restrictions!" Kara sounded almost hysterical with joy.

Kara…whose wedding was in a matter of weeks.

"So…you don't need me to be your bridesmaid, and speak at the ceremony?" Callie ventured.

"Of course I need you, silly! You're the only member of my family I trust not to mess things up. I mean, I love them and all, but I want it to be perfect. Anyone else would stumble over the Latin, and even Knut admits he bit his own tongue last time he tried to get the Norse right. But instead of just ten of us, we can invite everyone! Well, everyone who's in the state, anyway, with the borders closed. I just checked with the wedding venue, seeing as that's what we originally booked, and they're fine with the additional numbers. In fact, they've basically said we can have the whole place to ourselves. So I've upgraded you to a suite, their second best room in the house. You should see the bed. It's as big as the one in the bridal suite. Tell me you're bringing a date to share it with. There's even space for two or three, if you wanted to…" Kara gave a wicked giggle.

Sharing a bed with one man would be challenge enough. Two or three sounded like hard work.

"Not everyone's as lucky as you and Knut," Callie said.

"Well, I know that, silly! That's why I'm marrying him. You are still coming, right?"

"Of course," Callie assured her.

"Because Uncle Lucius was asking about you, when he called to RSVP. I told him you're definitely coming."

Callie's heart sank. "Is…" She couldn't even bring herself to say his name. "Is he coming?"

"He is now. He's normally too busy travelling around with that team he coaches, but as all sports have been cancelled with the restrictions, he's promised me he'll be there. And he can't wait to see you!"

Fuck.

Kara kept talking, but Callie wasn't listening any more. She mmhmmed her way through the rest of the call, until Kara finally finished, when she managed to mumble a goodbye before her phone tumbled onto the desk from her nerveless fingers.

She'd take a zombie and a moth man and a vampire in her office right now over a wedding with Uncle Lucius there.

Callie snorted. Because imaginary monsters didn't exist, but Lucius was all too real.

Real or not, though, she'd promised Kara. She would be there for the wedding, no matter who else Kara invited. She just had to find a way to attend the event and defend herself against Uncle Lucius.

FIVE

It took Callie a week before she was game to try translating the black book again. A week of sleepless nights and lots and lots of calming herbal tea that didn't seem to be doing much. Yet, here she was in the staff kitchen again, brewing up an entire teapot of the new tisane she'd bought from the fancy tea shop.

Catena came in, looking like she'd had even less sleep than Callie. But the librarian had her own brand of insomnia, as Callie knew all too well.

"You been up late reading again? Was he hot?" Callie asked.

Catena just shook her head, her gaze fixed on Callie's tea pot. "What do you know about foundation sacrifices, and hiding shoes in ceilings?"

Well, that was a weird question. But evidently a serious one, or Catena wouldn't have asked it. It sure was more interesting than mythical monsters.

Callie grinned. "Are you planning on taking up dark magic? I think I have some medieval spellbooks on those things. Not for the faint-hearted, though – there are some pretty stomach-churning ingredients in those. Even the spells that don't involve corpses."

Not that they'd do anything, but it was still gross.

"Could you…could you take a look for me, and let me know what you find out?" Catena asked.

"That medieval magic was pretty fucked up? I can tell you that right now. Anyone who thinks killing someone to strengthen their walls instead of just building a better fucking wall has some serious issues. Makes Shakespeare look like Disney."

Catena fidgeted. "No, it's just that my neighbour found a pair of baby shoes in her ceiling, and if someone who believes in that stuff put them there, there's no knowing what else might be hidden in the house. It's more than a hundred years old, and...Callie, what if the original builder was a serial killer, only no one knew because the bodies are in the walls?"

The librarian had been reading too many murder mysteries, Callie decided.

Callie dismissed the idea with a wave of her hand. "Someone would have noticed people going missing."

"Not always."

Callie sighed, then poured herself a cup of tea. "All right, I'll take a look through some of my witchcraft texts and see what I can find.

Anything else? As long as it's not the Moth Man, I have time for a bit of research in the inter semester break." Or now, if it allowed her to procrastinate instead of translating the black book.

Catena hesitated. Then, all in a rush: "Gargoyles. Anything you can find about them."

Monsters. Why did it always have to be monsters? Then again, maybe Catena just meant the ugly gutter spout statues.

Callie ventured, "Okay. I've never heard of anyone having a gargoyle problem before. Rats, yes. Cockroaches, definitely. But gargoyles? I know they're ugly, but so's wallpaper, and people still buy that."

"Not all gargoyles are ugly," Catena blurted out.

Callie considered for a moment. "Okay, maybe some of the Disney ones are kind of cute, and there was that musclebound one who was pretty hot for a cartoon, but I think the whole point of gargoyles is to scare away threats. Pretty won't work for that."

Catena nodded mechanically. Like her thoughts were far, far away. Likely on whatever book had kept her up late last night. Unless…

Callie swallowed. She had to be sure. "Just checking…you want this info for research purposes only, because you're an archaeologist and you live in a historical site? You're not trying to summon something from the nether hells to protect your house from zombies, right? Because none of that stuff is possible. Trust me, I know. I have a library full of Latin texts with instructions on how to do those things, and not a single history text that actually says someone succeeded. I mean, witch burnings would've been a whole different beast if the witches had summoned demons to protect them, if you get my drift."

Catena actually smiled. "Nope. I'm all about banishing demons, not summoning them."

"Good." Callie breathed again. Then she checked her watch. "Now, tempus fugit...don't you have a library to open?"

Catena glanced at the clock. "Shit."

Callie probably shouldn't have laughed as the librarian dashed across the courtyard.

Then again, Catena had given her the perfect excuse to flip through the books she'd already translated, instead of the one waiting for her in her office.

Callie picked up her teapot and cup, and marched back to her office to get to work.

SIX

When Callie had pretty much exhausted all the sources at her disposal, she headed over to the library to find Catena. "Hey, can you meet me in my office when you get a minute?"

Catena jumped and stared at Callie in horror, as if she hadn't heard her come in. "What is it?"

Callie flashed a reassuring smile. "I hit the motherlode on those shoes of yours, but this stuff is dark. Lose your lunch dark, and that's just the stuff in English. In some of my Latin texts…that stuff will give you nightmares. Best I tell you everything in my office, with the door closed. Don't want any of the students overhearing, and deciding to try things out over the holidays. The best thing that might happen is they get arrested."

"Sure," Catena said. "I'll pop in when Emily, the girl working the evening shift, arrives."

Callie could only nod and head back to her office.

Where the black book waited…

"Fine," she growled, and began.

What seemed like only a moment latter, someone knocked at her door.

"I'm busy! Vitally important research project on a deadline!" Callie called. This was the demon summoning spell. It had to be.

"I'll come back tomorrow, then," Catena said.

No…wait…she had to talk to Catena…

Callie marched over to the door and threw it

open before Catena could leave. She grabbed her arm and yanked her inside, before slamming the door behind her.

Catena shrugged out of Callie's grip. "Vitally important project on a deadline, huh?"

Callie shrugged. "Well, it could be vitally important. I won't know unless I've translated it all, will I? So far it's all about how to summon demons and other magical servants, by opening doorways to other realms but no word on how to shut them again once you have. I think it's important to know how to close the gates of hell, don't you?"

"Who's this translation project for?"

Damn librarians. Too smart for their own good.

Callie grinned impishly. "You, of course. You did ask for stuff on foundation sacrifices. Doorways are just the beginning."

Catena sank into Callie's visitor chair. "Okay, hit me with it."

"All right, then! Well, the surface stuff you've probably found already. There's plenty of articles in the literature, and even a couple of theses. All recent, in the last decade or so. So if you're looking for something to put in a research or grant proposal for, you're in luck. It's kind of like the wild west out there – stake your claim, and hope it pans out."

Catena shook her head. "This is just a favour for my neighbour, and maybe a bit of my own presence of mind. I mean, we live in the same building, which is divided into two apartments. So if her half's cursed, you can be pretty sure mine is, too."

Callie clapped slowly. "Oh, you don't know the half of it! Curses, my sweet summer child, are nothing compared to the dark magic I've dug up. In fact…"

The door swung open, and one of the theology professors stood there, his glasses halfway down his nose as he peered down at his phone. "Callie, I need you to do some research for me. There's some sort of creature called a Moth Man, and all my students are asking about it. I must know which level of hell it hails from." He glanced up at her, as though expecting her to answer him on the spot.

Fuck. Not this again.

Callie rose from her seat and crossed the office to stand in front of him, doorknob in hand. "The bullshit level, Christian. Moth Men don't exist. Now, if you'll excuse me, I was in the middle of an important meeting…"

Professor Christian held out his phone. "But there's a video, and it's clearly a winged demon dancing! How can I have any credibility with my students if I can't identify all the demons in hell?"

Maybe if he taught something that actually existed…? Callie shook her head. She wasn't going to get into that argument again.

"I can't help you, Christian. I'm not an expert in demons, after all. Just the Latin lecturer. Now, if you want any texts you find in your research translated, then I might be able to help you, but I'm very busy at the moment, so you'll have to wait for a spot to open up in my schedule, same as everyone else."

Professor Christian glanced around the office, as if looking for someone important, before his eyes settled disapprovingly on Catena. "Aren't you the junior librarian? You must be able to help me find out about these things."

Catena opened her mouth. Then her phone buzzed. She held the phone up in both hands like it was fucking Communion. If it saved her from Christian, maybe it was.

"I really need to take this. I'll talk to you later, Callie!" Catena said as she left.

Well, fuck.

SEVEN

Waiting in the bushland behind the mill until darkness fell was abominably boring. Wystan and Harlow had actually stretched out and fallen asleep. Stan looked like he was plotting, too caught up in the anticipation of finally winning the woman he'd fallen in love with, and Grant…he wanted to do something, instead of sitting around on his arse like some useless lord in his castle.

Grant snorted. If he had a castle, instead of the cottage he shared with his cousins, he'd have girls flocking to become his bride. But then, he didn't want any girl. He wanted one with high spirits to match his own.

One who would…disappear into the bushes with him to help pass the time, before stealing into the mill by his side for this daring raid. One who would match him, adventure for adventure, standing beside him as his equal. Not one of the washed out drabs this colony seemed to make of its women. No, he wanted a spitfire, like one of those striped tiger snakes that would chase a man for miles if he so much as looked at it wrong.

A raven cawed in the tree above his head, proclaiming the tree as his territory. It was answered by an angry chittering, as a black and white streak darted in to attack it. It took Grant a moment to identify the streak, for it was so small and fast. It was one of those willie wagtail birds, less than a tenth the size of the raven, but what it lacked in size, it made up for in fearlessness.

Grant chuckled softly. Perhaps what he wanted was a girl like a wagtail, not a snake. Small and brave and fierce, but not venomous. Not someone who would turn on him, as Dana had, the daughter of the vicar who'd taken Grant under his wing to teach him Latin and all the other godly things he'd need to fulfil his mother's dream of him becoming a vicar himself. But it was beneath Dana's skirts he'd learned a whole lot of ungodly things, until Vicar Jordan had discovered his virtuous daughter was pregnant.

And the child wasn't Grant's, either, though Dana had allowed the vicar to think so. Grant had been unceremoniously kicked out of the vicar's house, while Dana was hastily married off to some old baron who'd lost his heir to Napoleon. Dana had visited the old man almost daily, so Grant suspected the child was actually his.

So Dana the snake had let Grant be tossed out like the contents of yesterday's chamber pot, so that she might become the lady in a great house.

He'd fancied himself in love, but the long ride home to the cottage he shared with Stan and Harlow had quickly cured him of that notion. No pains of the heart, or any such things assailed him. All he missed was her body twined around his, in the throes of passion, while his fingers tangled in her dark hair.

Yes, Stan could have his golden-fair lady, who worked diligently all day, keeping house for her brother. Grant wanted quickness, and bird-bright eyes beneath dark hair.

What he'd give for such a woman now, for it had been years since he'd lay with someone who could tempt him. Damn, now he was hard as a rock, just thinking about Dana. Well, his hand would have to do, like it did most other nights since he'd arrived in the colony.

"Where are you going?" Stan asked.

"To relieve myself," Grant replied, heading deeper into the bushes.

One day, he'd have a raven haired beauty of his own, a bride worth stealing. Until then…he had two hands and a fervent wish he would find her soon.

EIGHT

Callie finished the translation. She'd known the black book was full of dark spells and rituals – including the demon summoning one she'd found – but seeing it all there, laid out in plain English, was worse than the spidery Latin script. Or the runes that looked like they'd been written in blood.

Then, like the good researcher she was, she went through the book systematically, looking for anything else she could give to Catena, when she returned.

Days passed, but no Catena. Callie went to ask in the library, but Lillian, the head librarian, only said that Catena had taken personal leave, and wouldn't say why.

So Callie went looking for a date to take to Kara's wedding. Only the selection on the online dating sites was positively dismal. Worse, now her inbox was full of hairy pricks they absolutely felt they needed to send her pictures of. From every angle.

Finally, when Callie fled to the kitchen to make a pot of tea, she spotted Catena.

"Where have you BEEN? You bolted out of my office like there were demons chasing you – though, I wouldn't put it past Christian to put them up to it, he knows enough about them – and then no one's seen you for a whole week!"

Catena swallowed. If anything, she looked ill. "I had to take some personal leave. My godmother died. I'm…I was her closest relative, so I had to make all the funeral arrangements. And then there was her will…she left everything to me. Her house, everything. I've been living there anyway, while she was in the nursing home, but now she's gone, it's…weird, wandering around a house full of her things, and knowing she'll never come back for them, because I'll never see her again."

Now Callie felt like a fucking slug.

"Well, unless you can raise the dead. Sorry, bad joke. I'm so sorry for your loss. That fucking sucks. I mean, I saw in the news that Maria Rennie had died, they had a full eulogy and everything, but I forgot that she was your godmother. No wonder you went into archaeology – she went everywhere, discovered so much! I bet she bequeathed you a whole bunch of artefacts, too. Stuff thousands of years old, imbued with all sorts of ancient curses…" If curses existed. Which they absolutely did not.

Catena shook her head. "Maria always said

what she discovered belonged to everybody. She didn't want to take things home, because she couldn't preserve them properly at home. She took pictures of everything, though – there's a whole bookcase full of slides. And every file had a picture of her with the dig teams, all the different places…"

"Ooh, speaking of digging things up, you ran out on me the other day before I could get to the good stuff. My office. Now." So she could tell Catena what she'd found in the black book, before burying it in the deepest, darkest folder on her computer where she never had to look at it again.

"I can't. I have to open the library in five minutes."

"Let Lillian do it. She's already there, and it won't hurt her. She didn't know when you'd be back, so I don't think she's expecting you today. So come with me and we can pick up where we left off when Christian so rudely interrupted." Please, Callie thought but didn't say.

Catena nodded, then grabbed her coffee and led the way back to Callie's office.

Callie's butt had barely touched the seat before she launched straight into it. The sooner she got this over with, the better. "Right. I told you all the dry stuff — the literature, and those theses — which I'm sure you found on your own. But it's the more obscure references where it gets really good. The first records date back to Ancient Rome, where one of the scholars describes the ancient Germanic peoples using captured enemies as foundation sacrifices. They'd bury the bodies under the lintel of their houses, ready to rise again to defend them when the next enemy attacked. Kind of like Romans raising armies among their conquered peoples, to go out and conquer more people…only the supernatural sort. Of course, while this Roman scholar saw the bodies being buried, he never saw them actually rise again and fight, so he chalked it up to superstition and that was that.

"Then I found some dark spell books, or at

least that's what they're supposed to be. According to the first few pages, they're the copy of a collection of earlier works based on the spells and rituals of Viking witches. Vikings being the seagoing descendants of some of those ancient Germanic peoples, and some Slavic ones, too, I figured it was worth a look, and I wasn't disappointed. Horrified, yes, and a bit nauseated, because these witches were into some seriously dark shit, but they actually laid out how they did the sacrifices. In among a whole lot of dark rituals for summoning demons and protectors and plagues and storms. Oh, and one to make a volcano erupt. Of course, you need a volcano for that one, and a whole bunch of weird ingredients. Plus a sacrifice. This book is big on human sacrifice. Though technically for the volcano one, you're supposed to kill a vampire."

Catena laughed. "Don't tell me you believe vampires exist now?"

"Of course not. And I'm not sure these witches did, either. They didn't call it a vampire, but a wretch who had drunk the blood of his own flesh and blood, so maybe they actually meant a cannibal. So, maybe it was actually a good deterrent for cannibalism. Don't eat the dead bodies, even if you're starving, or the witches will throw you in a volcano, and then it'll be worse for everybody."

They both laughed at that.

"Okay, but…the bit about summoning protectors and things. Can you tell me more about that?" Catena asked.

Callie winced. The one ritual she didn't want anyone to cast. The reason she'd stolen the book. But maybe if she told Catena about the other ritual, the foundation sacrifice one…that's what she'd asked for, wasn't it? And they were protectors…sort of.

"Funny you should ask, because that's the bit that matches the Roman scholar's account, though it goes into way more detail. Okay, let me find the exact page and I'll paraphrase for you. Here it is. There's a lot of steps. First, you have to find an enemy. The stronger, the better, because they make better undead defenders. Then you make him drink some sort of herbal tea. I couldn't translate the ingredients, but whatever they are, they're supposed to put him to sleep. Then you cut out his heart...yep, his actual heart...or, wait. Maybe you don't cut out his heart, you just cut open his chest. Okay, well, there's cutting and after that, you place a stone over his heart or in the cavity where his heart was, and you sew him up again. The stone has to be the same as the place you want to protect. So, cut from the ground or the same sort of stone the walls are made of, I think.

"Okay, so you have this poor drugged bugger with a stone stuck in his chest, either dead or soon about to be, and you bury him under the threshold. If you have a whole army of them, you're only supposed to put the strongest one, the leader, under the threshold, and the rest beneath the walls of the place you want to protect. And that's how you make a foundation sacrifice."

"That's it?" Catena blurted out.

Callie laughed. "Well, if you're into backyard surgery and burying people alive, yeah. Oh, wait, there's more…there's a whole second set of instructions on how to summon them when you need them. You're supposed to lift the cover stone – the threshold, or whatever they're buried under. Then you summon them to protect you." She peered at the screen, checking to make sure she hadn't missed anything. "Actually, that's all there is. The next page is all about summoning a demon protector, which looks like it uses the leftovers from the first ritual, because you need a fresh heart. Oh, ewww…." Callie shuddered, hoping Catena wouldn't ask for that one.

"But isn't there anything about how you…un-summon them?"

Callie shrugged. "Nope. I guess once you've done all that work, you wouldn't want to. And if you did, you'd probably just dig up the body and burn it. Well, unless you've woken the warrior up. Then I guess you're stuck with him." Well, if it were actually possible, and magic existed.

"Did you find anything about gargoyles?" Catena asked.

"In this book? Nah, they weren't big on churches, these witches. Oh, I did run across a story about a gargoyle who seduced a nun, or she seduced him, and they ran away together. Something about her love freeing him from his vigil, melting his heart of stone, so he could climb down from the roof and…well, do what gargoyles and nuns do when they've been lonely for a long time. Maybe that's why the witches used enemies in their protector summoning spells, because it's pretty hard to melt the heart of someone who wants to kill you." Callie managed a smile, hoping she'd steered Catena away from demons for the moment. Hopefully forever.

Catena blew out a breath. "So, basically, the only way to free a protector from servitude is to melt his heart of stone? Take a blowtorch to him or something?"

As if she had an actual protector she wanted to free. No, that couldn't be possible. It just couldn't.

Callie tried to make light of it. "Well, from the sound of the story, it was more of a metaphorical melting. It was a romance, after all. I imagine they probably had a few drinks, maybe shared a meal together, watched a minstrel show, he caught a glimpse of her with her hair uncovered through her chamber window and…well, gargoyles are naturally naked anyway, aren't they? Maybe he watched her from his rooftop for ages until finally he snapped. He hopped into bed with her and bam! She sucked him in with her magic pussy and freed him from durance vile!" Callie shrugged. "He doesn't sound so different to some of the guys I've dated. They start out all grumpy, but get a bit of food and alcohol into them, maybe even a suggestion of sex, and the sunshine comes out. Well, sometimes more arsehole comes out instead, and then there's no second date, but who wanted one, anyway? Online dating sites are a waste of time. I should try summoning a demon protector. I'm sure there's some fresh hearts in the medical school labs. It's not like I'd actually need to kill someone..."

The idea sounded better and better. The spell probably wouldn't work, but then again, online dating sites weren't working either. Maybe...

She was vaguely aware of Catena thanking her and saying goodbye. She thought she managed to mumble an appropriate response, before diving back into the translation. Maybe this wasn't such a crazy idea after all...

NINE

It was Christian this time, Callie was sure of it. She hadn't helped him research Moth Men, so he'd told the faculty head she was hiding one in her office, and now they were exorcising the place again.

So she stomped off to Tacey's coffee shop, where at least she wouldn't have to listen to stupid men whining about non existent monsters.

She'd just sat down with the biggest cup of hot chocolate Tacey had on the menu when the strangest sight appeared.

One of Tacey's staff…Rochelle, Callie thought her name was, staggered down the steps from the upstairs apartment. She'd heard about girls walking like that after a shipload of sailors had been in town on shore leave, but this was the first time she'd actually seen it.

"Who have you been riding so hard he's made you bow-legged? I want his name and number," Callie blurted out before her brain had caught up with her mouth. There couldn't be any ships in town, with the borders closed. Still, that meant there were still plenty of men around who couldn't leave the state. "He's got to be good if you can barely walk after." More to herself than to the others. "Unless it was something not good and I need to cast a curse on someone. I know some good ones." Callie wiggled her fingers.

Rochelle looked alarmed, like most people did when Callie threatened them with magic. If only they knew…

"No, I haven't heard from Jakob since I left him," Rochelle said, not sounding the slightest bit upset about it, either. Good for her. "Ben came to visit last night. He wanted to build his portfolio and I offered to model for him. So many poses…we were at it for hours."

So the stallion's name was Ben, was it? "Oh, I don't doubt it. So, did you go through much of Octavia's condom collection?"

Rochelle's cheeks turned red. "I…"

A muffin landed so heavily on the table, Callie thought Tacey might have thrown it down. She was surprised the plate hadn't cracked. "Stop teasing her, or I'll tell her why you're here instead of at work. Ben's our artist in residence in the evenings at the café. If you want to meet him, come down any night. He takes commissions and he's evidently looking for more models to build his portfolio."

"And he's as virile as a bunny, evidently," Callie said, then bit into her muffin before Tacey could snatch it away.

"Honestly. Right, you asked for it." Tacey turned to Rochelle. "Callie's here because her office is being exorcised for the second time this month because someone thinks she's been summoning Moth Man demons and releasing them in Fremantle."

Callie shrugged. "Can't summon what doesn't exist. I did find a good demon summoning spell, though. It'd be fun to try, just to see what happens. The ingredients looked like they'd be hard to find, though..."

But she could find them, she was sure of it.

"Well, as long as the spell doesn't involve toilet paper and hand sanitiser, maybe we should try it on our next girls' night," Tacey said.

Actually, that might not be a bad idea. If they all tried it, as a bit of a laugh, maybe she wouldn't be so disappointed when it definitely didn't work. Then they could all get drunk together, and think up a better solution for Kara's wedding.

TEN

"Hey Callie, can you come into the café again soon?" Tacey asked as she sauteed something that smelled delicious in the frying pan.

"Sure. Am I forgiven for teasing your barista yet? The bow-legged one?"

"Huh? Oh, I'm sure Rochelle's forgotten all about that. We've been so busy, and she spends every spare moment with Ben when she'd not at work. He's the one who wants to see you."

"For sex? Is Rochelle not enough for him?" It was only half-hearted, though. Callie wasn't sure she was quite up to sleeping with a man with that kind of stamina.

Tacey made a derisive sound. "He was asking about your translation skills, actually. And something to do with gargoyles. But you should know he's pretty much appointed himself as Rochelle's bodyguard, keeping the undesirables away or at least in check. He is a wonderful artist, too. He wouldn't tell me what he needed translated, just that he needed to speak to you."

Callie shrugged. "Sure, why not?"

ELEVEN

Callie placed her order with Rochelle, before scanning the customers. "So, which one is your artist in residence?"

Rochelle didn't even glance up from the coffee machine. "Ben won't be here until after sunset. Something about the light. But when he does arrive, that table is reserved for him." She pointed to the table in the corner.

"Then that's where I'll sit to wait for him."

Callie didn't have to wait long. And the weirdest part was, she knew him the moment he walked in the door. There was something…different about him. Which sounded strange, because he looked like an ordinary university student. Only…he wasn't.

She jumped to her feet and stuck out her hand. "I'm Callie."

Ben took it. "Ben Stone."

Callie gave herself a mental shake. There was nothing magical about this man. He was just young and hot, that was all. "The unusually handsome artist in residence at the Shut Up Café, and Rochelle's new ride, if the rumours are to be believed." She winked.

Ben offered her a polite smile. "I'm sorry, I don't understand," he said. A lie, if Callie wasn't mistaken.

Definitely not a student. Not with those manners. "Ooh, a gentleman! Goddess knows she deserves one, after that gaming arsehole. And she keeps looking over here, like she thinks I intend to steal you. Well, you make sure you tell her I wish you both the best together. But you didn't invite me here for my blessing, unless you wanted it done in Latin. Tacey said you were interested in gargoyles."

Ben nodded and leaned forward. "I was talking to Catena, and she mentioned you had some sort of spell book that said how to turn people into gargoyles."

Truth.

Callie said, "It also says how to summon demons, make a man perish of lust, and ward a house from evil spirits, but there's no evidence to prove any of these things are even possible, let alone that the instructions in this book would result in the desired outcome, even if it was. And if you even think of casting any of these spells on Rochelle, or anyone else I know, I must inform you that I know some particularly nasty curses and I will cast every single one of them on you."

He looked intrigued, instead of scared, like a normal person would. "What kind of curses?" he asked.

Callie thought fast. "I will curse your phone so that all the text appears in Ancient Greek. I will curse your nostrils so that you will smell nothing but ammonia for a week. And I will poison the mind of any woman who thinks to bed you, so that they believe you are infected with a deadly strain of genital herpes."

Ben relaxed. There was definitely something different about him. Everybody recoiled in disgust at herpes. They didn't relax, or remark, "I wouldn't mind brushing up on my Ancient Greek. I did have a classical education, but I admit I have forgotten much of my Greek and Latin. But Catena told me you were fluent in both Latin and Viking runes."

Not a single lie in any of that.

Callie sighed. "You're an arcane history buff like Catena, aren't you? All right, I brought scans of the book, and my translations. They're all on my laptop. In the meantime, I'll give you the short version I gave Catena…"

She was forced to break off when Rochelle appeared. "Hi, Rochelle! Are you coming to the girls' night Tacey has planned for next week? It'll be at Alethia's place so as not to wake up Rory, like we did last time."

Rochelle shook her head. "I'll be working, either here or at the prison. You all have fun, though. Is there anything else I can get you? Another muffin, maybe?" She looked from Ben to Callie, but they both shook their heads. "All right, just let me know if you change your mind." She collected Callie's empty cup and plate and left.

"Please tell me you're not going to leave her hanging," Callie said. Because if he did, she was totally going to ask him to come to Kara's wedding and be her protector for the weekend.

Ben stiffened. "I assure you my attentions toward Rochelle are purely honourable."

Of course he was taken. "Yeah, yeah. She could do with a bit of honourable after the last bloke, but I'm just saying, you should make sure it comes with a big side order of dick. Good dick." The sort of mythical, unicorn dick Callie was pretty sure only happened in books.

If only…

Ben nodded, as if he could read her mind.

Callie asked, "Well, what else did you want to know about foundation sacrifices? Except that they sound seriously gross and twisted, and anyone who does them has some serious issues?"

Ben shuddered. "Yeah, cutting into bodies like that would take a decidedly twisted mind. I can understand why they'd choose to do it to their enemies. I couldn't imagine doing something like that to the bodies of your family or friends, or anyone you cared about."

Callie's heart turned to ice in her chest. "Please tell me you are not going to try to make a gargoyle, or I swear to you, I will make good on those curses, only I'll swap out the Greek for kanji and then you'll be sorry!" Because while mythical monsters might not exist, a man who cut out someone's heart was a very real monster in her book.

Ben raised his hands in surrender. "I have no intention of sacrificing anyone. But I have seen…where it was done. Once. It was not pretty." More honesty, as was the horror in his expression.

Interesting. Callie was dying to ask for more, but she sensed he didn't want to give any more details about what he'd seen. She could respect that. She wouldn't want to recall dismembered corpses, either.

She checked her watch, then pasted a bright smile on her face. "Well, it's been fun, but it's my turn to cook tonight, so I should be going."

He was polite as he said goodbye, but Callie thought he looked relieved to be rid of her.

TWELVE

Finally, darkness had fallen, and Stan had led the way down to a clump of bushes close to the mill. They'd watched his bride bank the cookfire and duck her head to enter the shabby tent that was no place for a lady to live. The cottage they shared was a palace compared to this. Damn William Steel for subjecting any woman to such degradation.

If he'd had a sister, Grant would never have

allowed to her to live so. He would have built her a cottage with his own hands before he'd let her live in a tent. But all William Steel had built was a mill, leaving his poor sister to sleep under frayed canvas.

Stan wasn't just stealing a bride tonight. He was saving her.

And William Steel deserved to lose everything tonight. So much for the uppity lordling he'd been in Scotland – here in the Swan River Colony, more worthy men like Grant, Stan and himself might rise to their rightful place. To show the world they were better men, deserving of brides like Carline Steel, who would have been denied them back in Scotland.

"All right, just like we agreed. We three see what is in the mill, while you, Stan, go steal yourself a bride," Harlow said grimly. He looked like he wanted to scrap the plan altogether.

But Stan needed their help, so Grant would not allow it.

Crouching low, Stan darted off between the trees, circling the campsite so he might approach the tent from the far side.

"Now," Grant said, breaking from cover to creep toward the mill.

"No, you fool!" Harlow hissed, reaching for him.

"We're no help to him hiding here! We must go to the mill!" Grant said, quickening his steps.

"But there's someone up there. A light. I can see…"

BOOM.

Something powerfully strong crashed into his chest, throwing him down on his back as it knocked the breath from him.

Couldn't…breathe…

"Grant!" he heard Harlow shout.

"Stay hidden. There's a man with a gun," Grant tried to say, but no sound came out. He didn't have the air to breathe, let alone shout a warning.

Then the rifle boomed again and everything

went black.

THIRTEEN

A crushing weight, forcing her down so she couldn't breathe. Pain, unbearable pain, that felt like it was splitting her in two, when she didn't even have the breath to scream…

Callie shot out of bed, grabbing the bottle of holy water that lived on her bedside table, ready to drown the demon that had been sitting on her chest.

Only…there was no demon. No one in her

room but her.

That's because demons didn't exist, she told herself. Just a bad dream. A ghost of a memory that she should have forgotten by now. It had been months since she'd had nightmares like this, and now this was the second time this week.

If someone hadn't cursed her with a paralysis demon that sat on her chest while she slept – and she had three different spells that purported to be able to summon such a creature – then it had to be worrying about Kara's wedding that was doing it.

Or, more accurately, the wedding guests.

Callie sank down on the edge of the bed and buried her face in her hands. The only monster she was afraid of was a human.

Uncle Lucius.

If it had been anyone else, she might have begged off attending the wedding. But this was Kara, and she'd promised to say the blessings she and Knut wanted. Even if she broke both her legs, she'd still drag her aching body up to do this for Kara.

Maybe she should ask Kara to uninvite Uncle Lucius.

But then Kara would want to know why, and Callie couldn't…couldn't…

Magic doesn't exist, Callie reminded herself. There's no such thing as demons or any mythical monsters.

Yet all these years later, she still couldn't bring herself to talk about it. Because if there was even the tiniest chance that she was wrong…

And she couldn't tell Kara. Not this close to her wedding – she had enough to worry about.

So uninviting him was out.

Which meant…she'd have to face him.

Preferably from behind a wall of muscle that glowered at him if he so much as breathed in her direction.

Callie closed her eyes. What she needed was a bodyguard. A protector, like Ben was to Rochelle in the Shut Up Café.

Like she could afford one on an academic's

salary. Not to mention if she brought a bodyguard along to Kara's wedding instead of a date, Kara was bound to ask questions, and Callie would end up telling her, and…

So she couldn't have a professional bodyguard, either.

If only demons existed…and she could use that spell to summon one to protect her. A demon would deter him, surely.

Callie snorted. She knew she was going mad, if she was even considering finding a magical solution to her problems.

A more sensible thing would be to go back to sleep. She'd have forgotten this insanity by morning.

FOURTEEN

"You are coming to the girls' night, aren't you?" Tacey asked. "We need a real show of force, if we're going to scare Alethea's stalker away. You know you're the scariest of the lot of us."

Callie looked up blearily from her breakfast cereal. The girls' night was tonight? She needed to pick up ingredients…couldn't do the spell without ingredients. Which meant calling in some favours from the medical school…

"Callie! Are you coming or not?"

Callie shook her head. "Of course I am. Wouldn't miss it for the world. We're going to protect Alethea like no one's ever been protected before. That stalker will run away screaming like a little girl."

Tacey smiled uncertainly. "You have a real doozy of a curse in mind for him?"

Callie forced herself to smile back. "Even better. I have a summoning spell I'd like to try."

And if it worked, no one would be more surprised than her.

FIFTEEN

From the look on Alethea's face when they arrived at her apartment, Callie knew this was a mistake. But it was too late to back out now.

"Are we going dancing?" Alethea asked.

Tacey rolled her eyes. "Oh, I'm going to let Callie explain this one. Especially as you'll have to dress up, too. I haven't worn these pants since before Rory was born. I'm surprised they still fit."

"I'm not," Octavia said, pushing past her sister to enter the apartment. "You spend all your time cooking in the café, so most days you forget to eat. After eating camp food for the last few weeks, I'm surprised I haven't gone up a size." She tossed her hair, so the iridescent green streaks caught the light. They'd been silver this morning.

"Yeah, yeah, you're both turning into whales," Callie said. "Next thing you know, the fridge will be full of krill." She eyed Alethia's jeans and bulky sweater. "You should probably get changed, by the way. Think warm, but dark and sexy."

That'd give her a moment to work up the courage to explain her crazy plan to Alethia. Tacey and Octavia had already told her it was insane, but they'd also said they were up for something crazy. And to be fair, this wasn't even the craziest thing they'd done on a girls' night.

Tacey cracked open the vodka, and they were well into their first glass by the time

Alethia returned to the lounge room, dressed to go clubbing.

Callie raised her glass. "Now if you don't look like the perfect package of demon bait, I'll offer myself up instead."

"Wait…what?" Alethea stammered. Wow, the stalker really had her scared. Normally Alethia would laugh when Callie mentioned magic or monsters or anything else non existent.

"Tell her, Callie," Tacey said tiredly. She handed Alethea a glass. "Have a drink first. You'll need it."

Alethea took a gulp, then nearly choked. "What's wrong with mixers?" she rasped.

She'd gone soft, housesitting for her parents instead of living with the rest of them in Bell House. Well, a demon summoning would harden them up better than a cup of concrete, or whatever that stupid line was.

Callie giggled. "You evidently haven't been buying much at the liquor store lately. There are limits on how much you can buy. One carton or two bottles. And no self respecting demon is going to come near a passionfruit premix, so I got the vodka. I want this to have the best chance to work, you see…"

No, she didn't.

Yes, she did.

She didn't.

Or maybe she did…

Tacey waved her hand, indicating for Callie to continue.

Right. She should be telling them her crazy plan, not arguing with herself in her own head.

Callie took a deep breath. "Okay. I found a spell book which may or may not be the genuine article. I have it on good authority that one of the spells may have actually worked and if there's any time to test it, it's when we actually need the help. The plan is to summon you a demon protector, who will stick around to scare off your stalker for as long as you need him, and then you just send him back to hell. The demon, I mean."

Before anyone could talk her out of doing

this, Callie pulled out a sheaf of papers from her coat pocket and began to pass them out. "I've translated the spell as best I could and printed out copies for all of us. Traditionally, it's done by one really powerful witch, but it also says in the book that a coven of four or more women – yes, it definitely says women and not witches – will have the combined power to perform spells, with the right ingredients." She lifted the cooler box onto the coffee table. The one she'd had to smuggle out of the medical school labs under her coat. After promising the lab tech a charm that would keep her house free of cockroaches. "Now, traditionally, the ritual is done skyclad, which means naked, but I figure seeing as it's winter and we're trying to summon a demon, dressing sexy and showing a bit of skin should be enough."

If anything would be enough. This was a terrible idea. They should just stay here and finish the vodka and find some other way to keep Uncle Lucius away from her.

Tacey drained her drink. "I still find it hard to believe you found a spell that worked. You're always the first person to say magic doesn't exist."

Callie blew out a breath. "I know. Magic doesn't exist, or I didn't think it did, but I was talking to someone recently who led me to believe it might. Maybe."

Tacey's eyes narrowed. "Is that what you were talking to Ben about? Seriously, Callie, he's a fantasy artist. He mostly does portraits while he's the artist in residence at the café, but I commissioned him to do a series of cartoons where the Moth Man comes in for coffee or muffins or…he even had him doing the dishes in one, because he'd forgotten his wallet and that was the only way he could pay for his coffee." She shook her head. "If he drew you a demon, he made it up. Much like the Moth Man, demons don't exist. Ask Rochelle. She'll show you the unedited video."

Alethea's eyes widened. "I should come down to the café, and see if he can draw me as an elf or a dragon or something."

"He only works evenings, but, sure, come in whenever you like. I should warn you, he has a thing for Rochelle, though, so he's kind of already taken," Tacey said.

Callie laughed. "Pity, because that guy's got to be the epitome of good dick, if you see Rochelle in the mornings. You can tell when she's spent a night with him, because she's practically glowing with best-sex-ever vibes in the morning." A real unicorn, that Ben. If unicorns existed. "What? At least someone's getting some."

But they'd picked up the pages of the translated spell book, and started to read, so no one heard her. Callie shifted uncomfortably in her seat. If they read it thoroughly enough, someone was going to get squeamish and say they shouldn't do it. They'd probably be right.

Alethea spoke first. "We're supposed to find consecrated ground, under the light of the moon, then place a heart still moist with the blood of our kin in a circle of salt and candles and runes, then say the right words to summon the demon, who will then consume the heart." She looked up, wild eyed with panic. "There is absolutely no way I'm going to let you kill someone to cast a spell that probably won't work just to scare off my stalker!"

Callie grinned. "Relax, I didn't have to kill anyone for it. One of the lab techs in the School of Medicine owed me a favour, so I figured it was time to call it in." She opened the cooler with a flourish.

"Callie, you didn't!"

"Is that really a…?"

"It's a pig's heart," Callie said quickly. "The first years dissect them, and the abattoir sends them by the bucketload. The rest of the pig's probably already been turned into sausages and steaks, so it's not like we have to dispose of a body or anything."

Octavia snorted. "Yeah, but not even a demon's going to believe that pig was a member of your family."

She had a point.

"Uh, yeah, there's no getting around that part. So, I brought some micro lancets – sterile ones – so we can each prick a finger and drip a couple of drops of blood each on the heart. We're all family, so that's the kinsblood sorted, and no one has to die." She looked around. "Come on, one quick prick and it's done. Best if we do it here, so we can wash up and put bandaids on and stuff, because there's still the salt, and I have a bottle of pig's blood for the runes. We just need to find consecrated ground. I was thinking maybe outside the cathedral…"

"The cemetery. It's all consecrated ground, with a church and everything," Alethea said.

Oh, fuck. They were really doing this.

Callie grimaced, and hoped it looked enough like a smile that no one noticed the difference. "That's the spirit! How far away is it?"

"Only a little way down the road, but the main cemetery is all fenced off, and the gates are locked. We'd be better off at the dig site.

It's still part of the cemetery, but I know the security code for the key, and the ground is already cleared, so it'd be a lot easier to do on bare sand, and just brush away the evidence afterward."

Callie nodded. Doing this with the girls was way better than trying the ritual alone. Well, the advantage of doing it alone was that no one would know when it failed to summon a demon, but with their help, she'd know she'd done the best she could to actually make it work. Conclusive evidence that magic didn't exist, if they'd done everything right and didn't have a demon to show for it.

"If we're going to do this, I vote we get dinner afterwards, because there's no way I'm going to be able to keep anything down if you expect me to paint with actual blood," Tacey said.

Callie almost laughed. Tacey butchered a fresh Christmas turkey every year – she didn't shy away from blood normally. Then again, it wasn't like she usually painted with it…

Callie nodded. "All right, so here's the plan. We go out to the graveyard, perform the summoning ritual, give the demon time to get here if he's coming, and if he's not…well, we'll know for sure that magic and demons don't exist, and we can come back here and pig out on pizza and finish off the rest of the vodka, while we watch Sam and Dean hunt monsters and stuff, because watching Jensen Ackles' butt always puts me in a better mood."

"And if Alethea's stalker turns up?" Octavia asked.

"Then we threaten to make him part of the ritual, and scare the shit out of him," Callie said. If only that would work on Uncle Lucius.

Best not to think about him now. They had a demon to summon…whose first job would be to scare away Alethea's stalker, before Callie took him to Kara's wedding as her date.

Oh, this was such a bad idea.

SIXTEEN

Looking at the flat expanse of yellow sand, it was hard to believe this had once been a graveyard, before Alethia and her team had started excavating it. Except…you could still see some of the graves at the other end of the site. Callie shuddered. Part of her wanted to go over there and peer in, to see if there was anyone in them, but the rest of her wanted to walk quickly away and forget she'd ever been here.

If only the other three girls weren't looking at her expectantly.

So Callie pulled out the translated pages, as well as the scan of the original book, and started setting up the ritual. The heart went in the middle, with concentric circles of runes around it, painted in pig's blood. She'd stuck a drop of her own blood in the bottle, too, just in case it would help.

Ah, who was she kidding? This was never going to work.

But if it did…

Callie mentally shook herself. If it did work, and they summoned a real demon, then it was important that every single rune was painted perfectly, with no mistakes. Because some of these were for protection, and if demons were real, she definitely wanted as much protection as she could get. For herself and her friends.

Because an uncontrolled demon was likely to be far more trouble than some ordinary human stalker, no matter how much the guy frightened Alethia. The picture in the book had looked like some sort of mutant, monstrous dog with horns.

Yeah, exactly the sort of thing she should take to defend her against Uncle Lucius. She'd have to tell Kara it was a new pet, an experimental new dog breed. Like anyone would believe that.

When the runes were all done, she set out the candles, lighting each one from its own match. They flickered in the breeze, but they didn't go out. Like they wanted to see if this spell would work.

The girls just watched her, passing the bottle of vodka between them.

Callie was definitely the designated driver tonight. None of the others could walk straight, let alone drive.

Maybe she should have hidden the vodka until afterwards. Oh well, it was too late now. "Right. Now we need to say the incantation. You have to be really explicit. Like: Demon, we summon you to enter this circle, so that you will help protect us. The original incantation was all singular – I command you to protect me – but as we're all doing this, we need the unity. The words aren't as important as the intention, and you have to be firm. Because if you summon and don't have control over it…bad things happen."

Funny, the book hadn't said what sort of things. She guessed the book assumed people would imagine the worst, and that's probably what would happen. Best not to tell the girls that, though. Instead, they should get this over with so they could go home and watch *Supernatural.*

"Okay, now we should all stand around the circle, holding hands, and keep repeating the incantation until something happens," Callie said. She held out her hands for Tacey's and Alethia's.

As if they'd planned this, they both gripped her hands like they expected her to pull them out of a pit. Better than being dragged into the pit.

Callie cleared her throat.

"We summon you, demon…" she began.

"…enter the circle…"

"…help protect us…"

"We summon you!"

"…help protect us…"

They started out together, but then Alethia began to chant faster, while Octavia droned, and pretty soon they were all out of sync, but that didn't matter. What mattered was they kept going. Kept the energy building, every time they said the words.

Callie almost thought she could feel the energy, humming through her bones. Like the spell had taken on a life of its own, and now it was using them, instead of the other way around. Over and over, she said the words, until she fancied she could see sparks flying in the air above the heart. Sparks where there was no fire.

Something beeped faintly in the distance, like someone pressing the remote for their car.

Alethea dropped her hand, breaking the

spell. As if on cue, a cold breeze blew every candle out at the same moment. "That's the security guard. Quick, make all this disappear, while I think of something to tell him."

They seized the still smoking candles, tossing them back in the box.

Alethea did a weird sort of Happy Feet dance on the circle, until Callie realised she was trying to scuff sand over the bloody runes, and she hurried to help her.

When the sand was smooth again, and the candles bundled up in Octavia's arms, all that was left was the heart.

Callie scooped it up, shoved it into a pile of sand, and smoothed it over. There. No one would ever know.

"Right, let's go," Tacey said. "Over the fence, before the security guy comes in."

"Can't," Alethea said from down on the ground. "I've twisted my ankle."

"What do we do?" Callie asked, looking to Octavia. She was the one with all the first aid training.

But it was Alethia who answered. "You three go over the fence, and I'll distract him, by asking for help. I'm the only one who's actually authorised to be here. I'll…tell him I forgot something, and came back to get it, then tripped and twisted my ankle in the dark. He'll have to help me, which will give you time to get to…ah, I only have one key, and I can't give it to you, or that'll look suspicious. Um…go to the car. I'll text you when I get home safe. GO!"

It seemed as good a plan as any. Not that they intended to go far. Callie, Tacey and Octavia exchanged nods, before they bolted.

Scaling the chain link fence was surprisingly easy. Maybe fear or something else had given them wings.

"We'll wait in the car, until Alethia tells us it's safe," Tacey said.

That…actually sounded sensible.

The car was warmer, too, than standing out here in the winter wind.

"Do you think she's okay?" Octavia asked,

hugging the box of candles to her chest.

"She works there, remember? She probably knows the security guard. She'll text us. And if she doesn't…we'll go and get her. Octavia, you can track her phone, right?"

Octavia shrugged. "Maybe. I've never done it before, but it can't be that hard."

They waited, and they waited. Until finally Tacey's phone beeped. "She's fine, she's home, but she's taken some pain pills, so she's going to sleep. She says have a drink for her when we get home."

Callie slumped. "So we're giving up on demon summoning and just going home?"

Octavia shrugged. "I'll summon Sam and Dean for you, and you'll have all the demons you ever need."

Yeah. Demons didn't exist outside of fiction, anyway.

But for a moment there, she'd dared to hope…

When Callie got home, she was definitely going to get into the rest of that vodka.

SEVENTEEN

Grant felt the call in his bones, before he heard it.

"Help protect us…"

He wasn't the only one stirring, either. There was movement in the dark. More men like him, readying to answer that clarion call.

The first of them burst upward, showering him with dirt as he felt a cool breeze on his face. For the first time in…too long.

Only other limbs were tangled with his, pulling him back down to propel the others forward.

And then the call fell silent.

No. He would not allow her to be hurt. He had to protect her!

With all his strength, Grant thrust his body up toward the light. If the others did not let go, he would drag them to the surface, too. No one would keep him from her.

Then the call came again. Quieter, yet more desperate. "Help. Someone, please help me."

Grant flapped his wings furiously and sped to her side.

Only someone else, with wings and horns just like his, had gotten there first, scooping her up and lifting her into the air.

Did she still need help?

No, she'd fallen silent once more.

So instead of attacking the gargoyle carrying her, he followed him. Until he landed on a rooftop, mantling over the girl like a protective bird of prey, and bared his teeth at Grant.

"MINE," he roared.

Grant banked, flapping furiously to hover above the gargoyle and the girl. Two others came to join him.

"We were summoned."

"Must protect."

The one on the roof just glared back. "There were four girls. Four girls, four protectors. She is mine. Go protect them!"

A vague memory floated to the surface of Grant's mind. Stan's bride. He'd stolen a bride. Grant would have to get his own.

He reached out, for the thread that connected him to the other girls who'd called. Three for three, though the girls were speeding away. Away from whatever had frightened them, and made them call for help.

"We must follow," Grant said, letting the thread guide him.

"They travel too fast," the man to his right panted. Harlow, his name was. Brother.

"Then fly faster," the one on his left snapped, beating his wings with a fury Grant could only envy. This was Wystan. He needed to protect more than most.

"I see them!" Grant cried, though what he could see was a mystery to him. The three girls were crammed into a sort of small, horseless carriage, moving faster than any horse could.

He grinned. But not faster than a gargoyle.

"The first to reach them gets first choice of the girls!" Grant declared, pumping his wings.

"Idiot. What girl would choose you?" Harlow grumbled.

Grant only laughed. This was destiny at work, magic at its best, guiding him to his greatest desire.

EIGHTEEN

There had been no clear winner, to Grant's chagrin, so they perched on the roof of the house the girls had entered, at Harlow's insistence.

"Because gargoyles go on the roof, of course!" he said.

On a cathedral roof, maybe, but not this slanted metal affair, rippled like waves on a beach. They must have looked like three glum, overgrown pigeons, all sitting in a row, to anyone looking from below. Bloody stupid, if you asked him.

"So how will we choose now?" Grant grumbled.

Harlow sniffed. "Well, it's simple, isn't it? Wystan will want the redhead, so he might protect her better than the lady he lost. You will choose the witch, for she will be the most challenging to protect, especially if she takes a dislike to you and casts a curse on you, which I have no doubt you deserve. Which leaves one woman for me. I shall take the sensible one, who carried the box of candles into the house."

Grant opened his mouth to argue. Only to close it again when Harlow's words sank in. "How do you know she's a witch?"

"She cast the spell that summoned us. Her friends helped, but it was her magic that made it work. Of course she's a witch."

Grant closed his eyes. Magic. Of course. She had to be the bride fate had in store for him.

He slid off the roof, and into the wall, as if the bricks were water. Searching for her.

He found her in a bedchamber, dressed in a tunic and trousers that hung loosely from her body. As he watched, she seized a chair and wedged it under the doorknob, before muttering an incantation that no one would enter her room while she slept.

Technically, he was already in the room, or at least its walls, so the spell did not keep Grant out, but he respected her wishes and remained where he was. He could watch over her from here. His witch.

NINETEEN

She couldn't breathe. So much weight, pressing down on her, so she couldn't breathe, couldn't scream, and the pain…

"Mistress, are you all right?"

The pain and crushing weight were gone, but the hand squeezing her shoulder remained. Then it disappeared, too.

A nightmare, Callie told herself. None of it was real.

"Mistress?"

That voice was real.

She fumbled on the bedside table until her fingers closed around cold metal. Throwing an arm up to shield her face, she hissed, "Back off or I'll spray you." Her thumb itched to press down and empty the can of pepper spray in his eyes.

"I meant no harm, mistress. You were having a nightmare. Quite distressing, it seemed, so I woke you. I am your protector, you see, and even if the danger is not real, when you call for help, I must answer."

She shifted her arm slightly, so she could see him. Well, the bulky shadow over by the door. Swearing softly under her breath, she flicked on the bedside lamp.

The can slipped from her nerveless fingers.

Probably a good thing, because pepper spray wouldn't work on that thing. She reached for the other bottle on the nightstand, and took a deep breath.

"Vade retro satana! Crux sancta sit mihi lux.

Non draco sit mihi dux. Vade retro satana. Numquam suade mihi vana. Sunt mala quae libas. Ipse venena bibas!"

He inclined his horned head, looking puzzled. "I'm not here to tempt you. I'm here to protect you. You summoned me, remember?"

The demon spoke Latin and English? Fine. She'd exorcise him in English, then, if the Latin version didn't work.

"Begone Satan. May the Holy Cross be my light. Let not the dragon be my guide. Begone Satan. Never tempt me with vain things. What you offer me is evil. Drink the poison yourself." She brandished the bottle of holy water, ready to unscrew the cap and throw it at him if need be.

"My tutor insisted it was, 'Get thee behind me, Satan,' but I think I like your version better. I mean, who knows what he'd do behind me? Begone is a much more sensible thing to say to the devil. Well, I think. I've never actually met him." He reached out and took the bottle of holy water out of her hand, then set it on the nightstand. "You might want to put that back where it was, in case he does turn up. I mean, you're obviously expecting him if you know Saint Benedict's exorcism formula by heart, in Latin and in English."

Callie swallowed. "So you're telling me you're not the devil? Even with the wings and the horns and the claws and everything? Because I'm not sure I should believe a guy who has a reputation for being the Lord of Lies, among other things."

The demon, or whatever he was, coughed out a laugh. "Me? You think I'm the actual devil? I'm no lord, mistress. Definitely not a devil, either. My name's Grant Steel. I was actually trained to be a vicar, until I…was called home to help out on the farm." He avoided her eyes and shuffled his feet. Not quite lying, but not entirely honest, either.

"Liar," she snapped.

His head snapped up, staring at her with hurt in his eyes. "I was trained to be a vicar."

Truth. He licked his lips with a particularly long, forked tongue. "Until…I was sent home." Also truth.

"Sent home to where?" Callie probed.

"My cousin Wystan's farm, of course. My brother Harlow and my other cousin, Stan, moved in with him after his wife died, to help him out, and as I had nowhere else to go and no other vicar would take me after the things Dana said…"

"Who's Dana?" Callie demanded.

She couldn't be sure, but it looked like his cheeks were turning red. A blushing demon? That was strange. He mumbled something and ducked his head again.

"I can't hear you."

He glared at her. "Dana was the vicar's daughter. Now she was a temptress. She seduced me, and the local lord, and heaven only knows how many other men before her father tossed me out and married her off. To the lord she'd wanted all along. She was already pregnant with his child when she seduced me, though I did not know it then.”

“A girl who seduced a demon? Please. Everyone knows it’s the demons who do the seducing!” Callie scoffed.

Now he really looked hurt. “I already told you, I’m not a demon. I’m a gargoyle. Your gargoyle protector, which you should know because you’re the one who summoned me. If you wanted a demon, you should have asked for one, though I doubt they’d be much good at protecting anyone. But if it’s a demon you want, fine. Dismiss me, mistress, and I shall be gone, just as you command.”

Callie closed her eyes and took a deep, calming breath. Then three more, just to be sure. When she opened her eyes, he was still there. Wings, horns and all.

She sighed. “When did I summon you?” Because she remembered trying to summon a demon, but they’d been interrupted, so one hadn’t appeared. Unless…

“In the graveyard, mistress. You and your three friends.”

Not possible. The spell had been interrupted. Couldn't possibly have worked. And yet…here he was, standing in her bedroom. Where he really shouldn't be.

She swallowed. This was six kinds of crazy, and she usually threatened to curse crazy before she had to deal with it. She wasn't sure any of her curses would work on this guy, though. "Right, Mr Demon," she began.

"Gargoyle. I'm a gargoyle, not a demon. And my name is Grant Steel."

"Fine. Mr Grant Steel the gargoyle, if you're really my protector, then you can go stand guard outside my bedroom door, and make sure no one gets in."

He grinned. "Of course, mistress. Ooh, I have an idea. What if I lie across your threshold as your faithful hound…" Before her eyes, he dropped onto all fours and began to change. One moment, he was a winged man, and the next, the wings were gone, and a giant hound stood in his place, tongue lolling out of his enormous fanged snout.

"No! No dogs in the house. If Salis sees you…no!"

With a faint pop, he was a man again. Well, sort of. He still had wings and horns. "Who is Salis? Am I to guard you against him?"

Callie couldn't help but laugh. "Salis is female, and she's the cat who lives here at Bell House. She does not like dogs. I've seen her chase off a German shepherd that would've scared me, if she'd have let it get close. If you see Salis, you be nice to her. If the stories are true, she's the last in a long line of mousers who keep this property vermin free, and have since Bell Cottage was built."

Grant, or whatever his name was, bowed his head. "I will protect your cat as though she were your good self, mistress."

"Callie. Call me Callie." Though she fully expected him to have vanished by morning, for this was surely just a weird dream, she was this close to dousing him with the holy water or even the pepper spray if he called her mistress again. Who did that?

"Yes, Mistress Callie."

"Oh, by the goddess…my name is Callie! Enough with the mistress already!"

"Yes, Miss Callie."

For fuck's sake. She pointed at the door. "Out!"

"Yes, Miss Callie." He stepped straight up to the wall, like it was an open door, and just…disappeared.

She waited for a long moment, but he didn't reappear. So she switched off the light and tried to get back to sleep. Sleep without nightmares and demons or gargoyles, naturally.

TWENTY

Tacey gripped her coffee mug with both hands, peering into it as if it held her salvation.

Callie was doubly glad she hadn't drunk so much last night. "Morning." She didn't dare suggest it was good until she knew how bad Tacey's hangover was.

Tacey sighed and set down the cup. "Morning indeed. Remind me never to go drinking in a graveyard with you girls ever again. I have aching muscles I didn't even know I owned from climbing that bloody fence."

"We should probably call Alethia. See how she's doing this morning. Whether her ankle swelled up like a balloon and she needs someone to come over and help her hop to the shower." Callie crossed her fingers that Alethia would be fine, because the only one of the cousins who'd had medical training was Sybil, and she was somewhere in the Arctic Circle, hoping to dig up dead Vikings.

"Already tried. Her phone went straight to voicemail. Ah, I'm sure she's fine. If she needs help, she'll call. She always does."

Which was why they'd gone out to the graveyard in the first place. To help Alethia, or try to.

"You didn't see anything strange last night, did you?" Callie asked.

"Nope. Except for us going to a graveyard for a girls' night. I didn't even see your new statue until this morning."

"What statue?"

"The one in the hall."

Callie headed back out into the hall.

How had she missed THAT?

He was huge. Horns, wings…everything she remembered seeing last night. Only this was definitely a statue, just sitting on the jarrah floorboards, in the hall outside her bedroom door, glittering in the sun streaming through the leadlight windows around the front door.

Callie swallowed. Either she'd dreamed him, or she hadn't. Or she'd seen this statue and dreamed he came to life…and had the gall to question her Latin translation. Bastard.

"Where did you get him? Did you find him in one of those bulk lots with old books? I mean, I can see why you'd want him…"

Callie didn't have an answer for Tacey. It just didn't seem real. As for why he was here…

"Why do you think?" Callie asked, pasting a smile on her face, as if her mind wasn't in complete turmoil right now.

"Well, it's obvious, isn't it? He's like the

God of Good Dick. I mean, with equipment like that, you'd want to ride him all night. Any girl would."

Callie looked down. And gulped. How had she not noticed before? It was sparkling in the sun, damn it. Like he was a vampire out of some teen novel.

"Gargoyles aren't supposed to sparkle," she said as she couldn't seem to stop her hand from reaching out and stroking…wait, how was the stone so warm? Sure, it was in the sun, but it was winter, and she could feel the cold floor through her slippers. He shouldn't feel so hot and smooth and…

"We should probably cover him up before Rory comes home. I mean, she's a bit young to see Michelangelo's David in all his glory, and your statue's way bigger than David."

Callie snatched her hand back. Yes, she didn't want to subject a six-year-old to demon dick. "I'm not sure we can get pants on him…do you have a kilt?" He'd had a Scottish accent last night, she remembered now. Odd.

"Maybe one of my old tartan school uniform skirts, but it's probably buried at the bottom of a box somewhere. Let me check the clean washing. Maybe there's something there…" Tacey vanished into the laundry. "Oh, perfect! Rory won't wear this any more, anyway." She emerged with a wad of pink and white gingham in her hands, then proceeded to sling it around the gargoyle's hips, before reaching around to tie it up. "There!"

Callie fought down the jealousy that threatened to boil over. She'd never been jealous in her life, and definitely not of anything Tacey had or did. She wasn't even sure she wanted to touch the statue that she'd dreamed had come to life in her bedroom last night. So why…?

"Oh, and these ended up in my washing. Yours, right?" Tacey tossed a scrap of black lace at Callie's chest, which she automatically caught.

Callie held them up. Yes, they were definitely her knickers.

And was it her imagination, or was the gargoyle staring hungrily at them?

Well, if he wanted them so much…

She flipped them over and tugged them down over his head, so the black lace covered his eyes. Between the undies on his head and the cutesy apron hanging off his hips, he wasn't anything to be afraid of any more.

"So, what's for breakfast?" Callie asked, heading back to the kitchen.

TWENTY-ONE

Tacey and Octavia left for the day, leaving Callie alone in the house. Well, except for the statue, of course, which she decided to avoid as much as possible.

She grabbed a couple of battered paperbacks from the box in the library and carried them out to the sunny, sheltered spot on the veranda that held a couch that must be forty years old if it was a day.

The first book was about a vampire hunter, and the second about a girl who was dating a vampire. Evidently the used book market was still big on vampires, no matter what anyone said. Which wasn't a bad thing, seeing as vampires couldn't possibly exist, so Callie was guaranteed a pure fantasy read from cover to cover.

And not a single glimpse or mention of a gargoyle at all.

She spent most of the day on the veranda, soaking up the winter sun in between trips to the kitchen for snacks and drinks. It wasn't until the sun sank behind the trees that she reluctantly closed the cover on the second book and headed inside.

To be greeted by: "I believe these are your undergarments."

She snatched the lace knickers out of his hand. "I believe I told you to stand outside my bedroom door and not move."

He grinned. "Yes, I did that. The sun helped. If the sun's rays hadn't turned me to stone, I certainly would have moved when you started stroking me."

Callie felt her cheeks grow hot. "You were a statue!" she hissed. She should never have touched him. Especially not there…

"Yes, but I see and hear and feel everything. I'm made of living stone. I should probably tell you I enjoyed it when you stroked me, and should you wish to do any further stroking, I'd be only too happy to return the favour." He winked.

For the first time in forever, Callie was actually lost for words. Most men sensibly backed off after she'd threatened them or told them to go away, and this monster was propositioning her. "You keep your pants on, or I'll use that pepper spray," she said.

His gaze followed hers down to…goddess, he was still wearing Rory's apron. With a definite bulge in the front.

"Yes, pants might be a good idea. If you have any that might fit me, I'd be grateful. This…apron only covers the front and little behind. In fact, your sister might have inadvertently squeezed one of my cheeks as she fastened it."

Jealousy burned through Callie again. "Tacey is my cousin, and she did not grab your arse." Even she knew it was a lie.

"I'm sure it was a mistake." Oh, now he was lying, too.

Callie closed her eyes and forced herself to take a deep, calming breath. Then another, just to be safe. "If there are any men's clothes here that might fit you, they'll be up in the attic. Bring back the apron when you're done, so I can wash it."

"Oh, you can have it now, if you wish."

Before Callie could protest, he reached back to untie the apron, and held it out to her. Then he turned, giving her the full moon view of his very naked backside, as he marched up to the nearest wall, and vanished.

"Fuck me," she whispered, balling up the apron and the undies. Actually, she should probably wash the knickers she was wearing, too, which were suddenly, inexplicably soaked.

TWENTY-TWO

The message icon on Callie's phone was lit up. Of course, it was from Kara.

YOUR DRESS HAS ARRIVED AND IT LOOKS AMAZING!!!! PICK IT UP ANY TIME.

She'd had the dresses all custom made by a company in Ukraine that did accurate period clothing. Clothing that required the right kind of underwear, so Callie knew it wasn't just one dress, but an underdress and corset as well as the actual gown people would see, all made to her precise measurements. Kara had wanted Callie to look like a Viking witch when she said the wedding blessing. Callie had considered arguing, but the moment she'd seen the dress Kara had in mind, she'd closed her mouth and just nodded. If it looked half as good on her as it did in the pictures on the company's website, she would wear it to death.

Maybe even to work, though the priests and religious scholars would probably try to exorcise her office daily if she did that, instead of just every other week.

She'd been looking forward to this wedding. Kara was the only non-Bell cousin Callie had ever been close to, and seeing her marry the man she loved was worth almost anything.

Except having to see Uncle Lucius again.

Just the thought of his eyes on her as she wore that beautiful dress made her skin crawl.

What she needed was a human shield. Someone who'd stand between her and Uncle Lucius for the whole event, so she never needed to look at him. She could just stare at the wall, when she wasn't watching Kara and Knut, and…

As long as no gargoyles stepped out of the bloody wall right in front of her, like this one had decided to do now. Almost like he knew she'd been looking right there…

"What on Earth are you wearing?" she blurted out.

He glanced down. "Trousers and a shirt. Just like you."

Callie pointed. "Those are bell bottoms. And that polo shirt is older than my dad. Seriously, you look like you stepped out of an episode of the Brady Bunch. Where did you get those?"

The gargoyle raised his eyes heavenward. "In the attic. There were pictures up there of men dressed like this."

Wearing similar clothes, maybe, but

definitely not like that. The polo shirt he'd picked clung to every ridge of muscle, all the way down, and the pants hung off his hips, showing off the faintest trail of hair, as if she needed reminding of the bloody obvious bulge in the front of his pants.

He looked like the pool guy from a 70s porno. Only…hot enough to actually get naked with.

A crazy idea popped into her head. "You should come with me to my cousin's wedding."

Because if he arrived looking like this, no one would even notice her.

"Do you need protection from your cousin?"

His eyes seemed to be reading her soul, as if every secret was laid bare.

Callie swallowed. "Not my cousin, no. But maybe the other wedding guests…" She would not say his name. Not even think it. Or the gargoyle would know, she was certain of it.

He bowed his head. "Then I shall stand by

your side at this wedding, and protect you. As long as it is inside a church, for in sunlight I turn to stone, and cannot move to protect you."

"Actually, the wedding won't be in a church at all, and it'll be at night," Callie said slowly, almost warming up to the idea. "You could stay inside during the day, and we'll say you're allergic to sunlight or something. I'm sure there's a woman at work who has an illness that means she needs to stay out of the sun. We could tell people you have that, and make sure you have shirts with long sleeves and maybe a hat. Or a really big hoodie..." She regarded him, trying not to let her gaze linger on the muscles that were...well, everywhere. "Maybe a hoodie and a hat, just in case. To hide your horns and..."

She blinked. "Where are your horns? And your wings?"

He shrugged. "I could not don this shirt with them, so I shifted into a more ordinary form. I can bring the horns back, if you wish, but I will need to remove the shirt if you want me to have wings…" He lifted the hem of his shirt, as if he wanted nothing more than to get naked again.

"NO!" Damn it, she'd soaked a second set of knickers already. What was with this gargoyle? No man had ever made her this hot. She took a deep breath, and managed a more even tone. "No, keep your shirt on, please. It's winter and people will think it's weird if you don't wear one. I'll just have to get you something more modern, so you don't look like Gilligan." Not that any of the men in Gilligan's Island had looked like… "You're going to have to tell me your name again."

"I am Grant Steel, Miss Callie."

She grimaced. "Just Callie. No one's going to believe you're my date if you call me anything but Callie. Especially if we're sharing a room, which we'll have to, because…" She swallowed. "Just because. If it were just Kara and Knut and close family, I wouldn't worry, but some of the older relatives will kick up a stink if we share a room and we're not married, or at least engaged. So…you'll have to pretend to be my fiancé."

As soon as the words left her lips, she regretted them. This was a terrible idea.

But Grant Steel did not seem to agree. Worse, he seemed positively delighted. "I would be honoured to be your betrothed, Callie. As your prospective husband, no one will question my desire to protect you. But surely I should find my own garments. It is a man's job to provide, after all."

Callie had to laugh. "Listen, Grant, I don't know what century you came from, but it's not the one you're in now. If a girl tells you she's going to buy you clothes, you shut up and say thank you, because you definitely need the fashion advice. If it means so much to you, you can pay me back later. After I've bought something suitable for you to wear to a wedding."

Yes, she was going to regret this. No, she

was already regretting it. But she'd take a gargoyle to Kara's wedding if it meant being able to avoid Uncle Lucius.

"Yes, mistress."

Callie sighed. What choice did she have?

TWENTY-THREE

Callie banished Grant from her bedroom again. This time, instead of standing outside her door until sunrise, he did a quick check of the house and, finding no sign of dangers she'd need protecting from, he headed up to the roof to keep an eye on the perimeter instead.

Only to discover Wystan was already there.

"It's easier to see threats coming from up here, isn't it?" Grant asked. He tilted his head to the side, stretching his neck, before doing the other side, too. "And the stars. I never remember the skies being this clear back in Scotland. Too much smoke."

Wystan looked up. "The stars are different here. We're a whole world away."

"A world and almost two centuries away, in fact. There is certainly some sorcery at work, for we should be long dead."

Wystan shook his head. "I, for one, am grateful my time has not come yet. I have a second chance to make good on what I failed at, back in Scotland."

Grant had to think hard to remember. "Protecting the redhead?" For that was Wystan's purpose here.

"The redhead and her daughter," Wystan corrected. He barked out a bitter laugh. "If she'll even let me in the house. She and the girl banished me up here. I'm not allowed in the house."

"Tacey," Grant said slowly, thinking back on the events of the morning. "She's good with her hands, that one. Tying an apron, cooking, or…other things, if you catch my meaning." He winked.

Wystan's fist closed around Grant's throat, squeezing. "Don't you dare speak of her like that. She is an honourable woman, not some doxy!"

"Easy, easy. I was only saying she squeezed my arse this morning, and she has a mighty firm grip. If you mean to make an honourable woman of her and protect her properly, I imagine you would like to know what sort of wife she would make."

Wystan only squeezed harder, cutting off Grant's air. Luckily, gargoyles didn't need to breathe, but he did need air to speak.

"Liar! She did no such thing!" Wystan roared.

Grant growled and twisted out of his cousin's grip, backing away to put some distance between them. "Women in this time are far more forward than the ones we knew, cousin. Why, I had both Tacey and Callie staring at my manhood, discussing it, as if such a thing were a perfectly normal discussion topic for unmarried women. Though if your Tacey has a child, as you say, perhaps she is married. What of her husband?"

Wystan shook his head. "There is no husband. She is an unmarried mother, I am sure of it. A widow would wear mourning of some sort, and she defends her daughter as fiercely as any lioness. She needs a protector, but I fear I have already offended her..." He sighed deeply.

Grant burst out laughing. "How did you manage to offend a woman who doesn't even blink at a naked man in her house?"

Wystan glared at him. "She might not mind a naked man, but she was most displeased to find a monster in her child's bedroom."

Grant nodded slowly. "That is fair. If I had a daughter, I would slaughter any monster who dared to even look at her. If one got into her bedroom..." He mimed ripping things apart.

"I tried to tell her I was there to protect

them, but she banished me before I could say more than two words," Wystan finished glumly.

Grant clapped him on the back. "Cheer up, coz! The universe is not so unfeeling as you think. You must only wait, and an opportunity will present itself for you to show her how good a protector you are. Then she will surely allow you in her house, and perhaps even her bedroom, where you will learn for yourself how strong her hands are, and how skilled. Then I shall be the one who envies you, for while Miss Callie has not banished me from her house, I fear she is not so forward as Miss Tacey. Though she does have a softer touch..." He was rock hard at the memory. Well, he was already made of stone, but... "While you keep watch from the rooftop, would you shout if you see anything we might need to guard against? Two of us are stronger than just one. Three or even four would be better, but...do you know where Harlow is?"

Wystan shrugged. "Protecting the woman

he chose. She departed in a horseless carriage and has not yet returned. I believe she fixes machines. A strange occupation for a woman. Perhaps she is not so ordinary as Harlow first believed."

Grant could only laugh. "Serves him right, then. Ah, may she run him a merry chase, then, that stubborn brother of mine. Meanwhile, I might go back down to check on Miss Callie. If you are all right to stand guard alone, coz?"

Wystan shrugged. "I shall stand guard here until dawn, before I will take shelter from the sun within the walls. You know where to find me, should you have need of me."

Grant inclined his head in thanks. "Then down I shall go."

He slid through the stone walls as easily as if they were water, instead of solid rock. It should have felt strange, but it seemed as natural as breathing. Grant rather thought he was getting to like being a gargoyle.

Callie's breathing was rapid, as if she was trapped in another nightmare. Indeed, she thrashed about in the bed as if at any moment she might cry out for help.

Then she did cry out, and Grant's mind went blissfully blank.

TWENTY-FOUR

When she was certain the gargoyle had left her room and was definitely outside, Callie stripped off and climbed into bed. She'd soaked through three pairs of knickers today, just looking at Grant the gargoyle, and it was getting beyond a joke. If she wasn't getting any real bedroom action from a man, she'd have to take matters into her own hands.

If she ever met a man who could actually

give her pleasure in the bedroom, or any other room…

Callie sighed. A man who gave good dick was rarer than dragons or unicorns. Or gargoyles, come to think of it.

She opened her nightstand drawer and reached for the bag at the back. The one that held the vibrator she'd never told anyone about, not even her housemates. She'd bought it one year when she was shopping for Octavia's birthday present, and the adult shop had just received a new delivery of them. The shop assistant had been raving about them to some rapt customers about how quiet and powerful they were, small enough so you could slip them inside and no one would even know you had them. Not like the giant dildoes lined up along the wall, as long as her arm.

Callie had bought three cartoon condoms for Octavia, and the silver, lipstick-sized vibrator that was probably about the same size as most of the men she'd slept with. Nothing like the monster jutting proudly from Grant's groin in the hall outside…

Was that what good dick looked like? How did something so huge actually fit inside a girl? Surely something so big would be painful, not pleasurable…

Which was why she'd bought a small vibrator, not a monstrous one.

Yet she couldn't help but wonder…what it would feel like…

She pulled the vibrator out of the bag, rubbing it against herself, but not turning it on yet.

Was this what his hands would feel like on her? He'd offered to stroke her, just like she'd stroked him, and maybe, just maybe, the mythical creature standing outside her door might be more than just a monster. Maybe…

The device warmed against her skin, until she could almost imagine it was one of the gargoyle's fingers. Sliding across her clit, into the wetness inside…

It felt so good, she'd barely flicked it on before an orgasm hit her.

What felt like forever later, when she could think again, she laughed to herself that no man had ever made her feel half as good as the thought of Grant the gargoyle.

Then again, he wasn't exactly a man, was he? Male, yes, but…some sort of magical, monstrous…something.

Something she wanted much, much more than she should.

So instead of putting the vibrator away, she kicked it up a notch, and rode it for a little longer.

TWENTY-FIVE

Stretched out across the back set of Callie's horseless carriage beneath a thick blanket that blocked out sunlight, Grant had little else to do but marvel at the smoothness of the ride as he listened to the music Callie had managed to make magically play in the vehicle, almost drowning out the bass rumble of the engine that powered it.

Some time had passed since he'd last walked

the roads of the Swan River Colony, Grant had discovered, and the machinery of this time was almost magical in how much it could do.

But even that couldn't drown out the memory that kept springing to mind, appearing behind his closed eyelids in the dark until he'd memorised every last bit of it.

They way her lips parted in an almost silent scream.

Her breath, panting so hard as her gleaming breasts heaved.

Her wet fingers catching the moonlight as they worked between her legs as she pleasured herself with the small, shining device that seemed to hum with smugness at being able to give Callie such joy.

And through it all, he still heard her voice in his head, though she hadn't said a word aloud.

"Yes…Grant, oh, yes, oh, by the goddess, Grant, again!"

He'd almost obeyed her mental summons a dozen times, nearly stepping out of the wall so that he could cross to the bed and give her everything she wanted and more.

She was the goddess, lying there, naked, consumed by her own pleasure. A goddess he wanted nothing more than to worship, day and night, for as long as he drew breath.

At least, she had been. Now, he could feel the tension rolling off her as she clutched the wheel with both hands, her thoughts little more than a litany of the same words, over and over:

I can do this I can do this I CAN do this I can DO THIS I can do this…

"Is it the wedding you're worried about, Miss Callie?" he asked finally, unable to bear such distress without doing something to help.

"No…"

"Your cousin, then? Do you not get along?" he persisted from beneath the blanket.

"Kara? Oh, no, we get along fine. Almost as well as I do with Tacey and Octavia."

"Is it her husband to be? Or his family?"

"No, Knut's everything I could hope for in Kara's husband. He's like…a fairy floss Viking.

Big and imposing and more than you think you can handle, but actually so soft and squishy he'd melt at one look from Kara."

"Who, then?"

A long moment of silence. Then, "My family."

Ah. That he understood. After all, they'd had William Steel and his father. Black sheep in any other family, if they hadn't inherited all the wealth there was, while the rest of the hardworking younger sons and sons of younger sons got nothing.

"I will protect you from anyone and everyone, I swear it. Even your own family, lass."

The next pause was shorter. "Thank you, Grant."

TWENTY-SIX

"Little Calliope!"

For the first time since he'd met her, Callie froze in terror.

Grant wasn't sure why. The man staring at her with rapt attention didn't look like he'd last three seconds in a fight. Grant would only have to sink his fist into the middle of that paunch and he'd be rolling on the ground, gasping for breath.

But he restrained himself – punching strangers didn't seem like a good way to introduce himself – so he wrapped an arm around Callie's shoulders instead and asked, "Who's this, darling?"

She pasted a smile on her face that resembled nothing more than a sick grimace. "This is my Uncle Lucius."

Paunch or no, this man had the power to frighten Callie. Which meant Grant was honour bound to protect her from him.

"Oh, good. Just the man I need to see. Will you help me bring Callie's things inside? You check in, darling, while your uncle gives me a hand." Grant's smile was as open and friendly as he could make it, which he knew meant the man could hardly refuse to help, or he'd appear a churl.

But Grant couldn't stop him from glancing back at Callie a dozen times before they'd even made it down the stairs to where Callie's carriage was parked.

Grant led the way in silence, waiting for

Callie's uncle to break it. The man didn't disappoint.

"I'm sure whatever stories Callie has told you about me are wildly exaggerated. She always had an overactive imagination. Demons down the bottom of the garden, and angels up on the roof." The man let out a nervous laugh that sounded awfully like a horse's whinny.

"Actually, Callie hasn't told me anything about her family, except that she had to attend a family wedding, and it might be a good chance for me to meet everyone before we officially announce our engagement."

The man's eyes bugged out like a toad that had been squeezed too hard. "Little Calliope, engaged? I never thought I'd see the day." This part was true, Grant judged.

Though why anyone who knew Callie well could imagine her as a spinster when she drew men to her with every breath, every look…

"You've got it bad, my friend," Lucius chortled. "She always was a temptress, was little Calliope."

Bile rose up in Grant's throat. This man was her uncle – he had no right to regard her so.

"Then you must not have seen her in a very long time. The Callie I know is an accomplished Latin scholar, with more knowledge of occult practices through the last thousand years than any man alive, including the professors at the university where she works. Why, she even puts me to shame! And makes me glad I chose to direct my studies elsewhere." Grant coughed. "The university does frown on student teacher relationships. Quite taboo, I understand."

The man flushed. Oh, by all that was unholy…Callie's uncle did harbour incestuous desires for his niece. No wonder Callie needed a protector.

Grant seized the first items he could find – a bulky dress bag and several sacks – and thrust them into Lucius's hands. While Lucius was still struggling to carry them all, Grant grabbed the remaining two bags and marched back up to the hotel desk, where an anxious

Callie stood waiting with a set of keys in hand.

"Quick, let's go up to our room before he follows us. We can come back for the rest," Callie said, trotting off so fast Grant had to speed up to keep up.

"Kara booked us one of the fanciest suites they had – the same as she and Knut, I think. They tried to give us one with balconies and a view, but I asked for something south facing, with thick curtains, so we don't get much sun. I mean, you have your hat and everything, but…"

Callie didn't want to be caught in the sun without her protector.

"Here we go." Callie unlocked the door, and led the way inside. "I'll close the curtains, and we'll keep them closed as long as we're here. I mean, it's not an issue now, but in the morning…"

These rooms were grander than anything Grant had ever lived in. Well, so was Bell House, but this was a great house that made Bell House look small. Grant's parents' cottage could have fitted inside the bedroom alone here, and there was a sitting room and bathroom, too.

"Put the bags in the bedroom," Callie instructed. "First I should hang up…where's my dress?"

"I gave it to your uncle to carry, to keep him busy," Grant admitted.

Callie paled. "Can you go and get it? I don't want him to know…"

Too late.

"I thought the bride and groom were supposed to get the honeymoon suite! This is much nicer than my room," Uncle Lucius said, puffing as he waddled into the room. The dress bag dragged on the ground behind him.

"Oh no!" Callie cried.

Grant rescued the dress from her uncle's sweaty clutches, before the man let the rest of her things fall to the ground as well.

"I'm going fishing later. You can come with me, if you want," Uncle Lucius said.

Callie began to babble so fast, even Grant

could barely make out the words. The only one he was certain of was the one ringing in her head: an emphatic NO.

"Maybe I will," Grant said. "But first I have to help Callie unpack. We'll see you later, I'm sure." He firmly ushered Callie's uncle out of the room, then shut the door behind him.

The both waited for a long moment, holding their breath, until the creak of Lucius's footsteps heading along the hall and down the stairs faded away.

Then Callie threw herself on the bed. "Fuck."

"I see why you need my protection. Your uncle wishes to have incestuous relations with you," Grant said.

Callie sat up in a hurry. "How do you know that? Did he tell you?"

"Not in so many words, but his every look betrays him. I swear to you, I will not allow him to touch you."

Callie managed a weak smile. "Oh, it's much too late for that."

Grant's mouth dropped open. "No!"

Callie swallowed. "I've never told this to anyone, and I won't let it ruin Kara's wedding. You have to swear you won't tell anyone what I'm about to tell you."

Grant nodded. "I swear I will carry your secrets with me to the grave. And beyond, if need be."

Callie took a deep breath. "Well, I was eight, and he arrived to stay with us on the night of my dance recital. We'd just gotten home, and I was still in my costume and makeup, when they arrived from the airport…"

TWENTY-SEVEN

"And afterwards, when I was lying on the bed in too much pain for his words to sink in, he said that if I ever told anyone, he'd summon a demon that would shapeshift to look just like me, and my parents would never know I'd been replaced by a demon instead of their real child. Another night, he showed me his spell book and pointed to the page with the demon summoning ritual in it. Not that I could read it then, but I still believed him. So I never told anyone."

Callie sucked in a breath. She'd thought telling Grant her deepest, darkest secret would make her feel dirty, like the first night Lucius had come to her bedroom and forced his crushing weight on top of her, and all the nights after. But instead, she felt…lighter, somehow. Like she should have done this years ago.

She smiled. A real one, this time. "Though I did get my revenge. One day, when he was in the shower, I snuck into his room and stole the spell book, then hid it. Then it was my turn to threaten him. I said I'd burn it if he ever touched me again, so he couldn't summon any more demons. And when I grew up, I'd learn to use the magic in the book, and I'd summon demons to come after him."

"You were only eight…" Grant looked gutted.

"Yeah, well, there's not much I can do about it now. It's not like I can change the past. I grew up, and learned Latin and Norse, and I learned to translate that damn book. I didn't believe in magic any more, so it didn't really matter, but I did learn that a lot of other people believe in magic, and curses in particular. And if you threaten to curse them, it's amazing how fast they back off. Not that I ever intended to try any of the curses in my uncle's spell book. Demon summoning isn't even the darkest thing in there. I'm still not sure how we summoned you, when we were supposed to be summoning a demon, though. I should probably take another look in there, when we get home."

Light dawned in Grant's eyes. "So that's how I'm still alive! Dark magic. I knew it must be something supernatural, for no man lives more than two centuries. I don't believe your uncle would have the power to summon even a gargoyle like me, let alone a demon. He's far too weak for that. Not like you."

Callie just shook her head. "He's twice my size now. And when I was eight…"

Grant's hands came down on her shoulders, before his lips pressed against her forehead. "Don't even think about him. He has no place in your head or your life now. I'm here to protect you, and he will never touch you again."

Tears sprang to her eyes. "Thank you!" She threw her arms around him.

Time stopped.

Slowly, she raised her eyes to Grant's face. Then her lips touched his.

She'd never known a kiss like it. Gentle and slow, giving her every chance to move away if she wished, but she didn't. Couldn't. Slow and insistent, too sweet to do anything but yield to him, matching him, until she could taste him.

He tasted like springwater, the pure, expensive stuff from the Alps, with the faintest hint of limestone from the rock that had purified it for centuries.

Only warm and welcoming and everything she'd ever wanted in a kiss.

Everything every woman who'd ever lived

wanted in a kiss.

And then…time started again. Callie's phone beeped with a text message from Kara, and her tummy grumbled like an angry cat, reminding her that it was dinner time. And somehow, she'd soaked through another pair of knickers again, which begged the question whether she should change before dinner or just head downstairs to the restaurant with Grant and hope no one noticed.

"There is a table and chairs here, with a menu for room service. It says we can order food to be delivered to your room, so you do not have to see him again. I shall guard the door," Grant said, moving away from her.

Callie swallowed. It was on the tip of her tongue to ask, no, to beg for another kiss, but the moment had passed, and she wasn't sure if it would ever return. Grant was here to protect her, like he'd promised. She should let him do that, so she'd be safe.

"Thank you," she said again, but words just weren't enough. Would never be enough.

TWENTY-EIGHT

Callie frowned at her phone. "Kara wants us to go down and meet them for dinner tonight in the restaurant."

"You don't need to go if you don't want to," Grant said.

Callie shook her head. "You don't understand. I've barely seen Kara for months, and this is her wedding. She wants to discuss details and she wants to meet you. I can't just say no."

"In that case, I won't leave your side," Grant promised.

She'd need to hold him to that. Even if every time he got close, she couldn't help reliving that perfect kiss…and wishing for another.

She swallowed and held out her hand. "Then let's go now, before I lose my nerve."

TWENTY-NINE

For some reason Grant could not fathom, as he took Callie's arm to escort her to dinner, he was reminded of all the dinners he'd shared with Dana and her father. The vicar had taken advantage of his captive audience to practice his sermons, but he'd also punished them if they yawned or gave him anything less than their full attention during his dull diatribes.

Then Dana had come up with a novel way

for them both to appear attentive. She had only to whisper, "Distract me," and Grant would…

"Grant," Callie hissed.

He blinked. A tall, blonde girl stood before him, with her hand outstretched. Without thinking, Grant leaned forward to kiss it.

The girl giggled, then pulled her hand back. "Well, he's definitely not ordinary. Not that you'd ever settle for ordinary, would you, Callie?"

The even taller man beside her threw up his hands. "Don't look at me. Vikings did handfasting, but not hand kissing." He held out his hand, and Grant shook it. "Happy you could come to the wedding, mate."

This must be Knut, which made the girl Kara, Callie's cousin. "Thank you for inviting me," Grant replied.

Knut snorted. "Kara's the one who made the guest list, not me. And I think she would've agreed to let Callie come with a giant sloth as her date, as long as she showed up for the wedding. Not that you look like a sloth. Shorter hair, nails, that sort of thing."

Grant couldn't help grinning. They might be standing in a grand house, but Knut was no fancy gentleman. Grant liked him. "Would you believe I've never seen a sloth?"

"You're not missing much. They smell terrible. I saw one at a zoo once."

"What did you see?" Kara asked.

"A smelly sloth," Knut said. "I think it was in Adelaide Zoo, when I was a kid."

Kara frowned. "I thought they had pandas there. I've always wanted to see a real panda."

Knut shrugged. "They just sit there and chomp on bamboo. But if you really want to, maybe we can go when the borders reopen again."

They moved into the dining room, taking a table with only seats for the four of them, though there were many other tables scattered about the room. The conversation continued along the lines of the various animals Kara, Knut and Callie had seen at zoos during their lives. Grant was fascinated. He only wished he could add to the conversation, but he had not seen any of the animals they spoke of. In fact, some of them he'd never even heard of before.

"What about you, Grant? What's the funniest animal you've ever seen at the zoo?" Kara asked.

Grant grimaced. "Actually, I've never been to a zoo. I have lupus which is triggered by sun exposure, and my mother did, too, so it's not something I ever got to do." Never mind that there hadn't been any zoos back where he'd lived in Scotland, or here in the Swan River Colony.

"You need to take him to see Perth Zoo. They open at night sometimes for special events. You should go then. Or Singapore Zoo, when the borders reopen and we can all travel again. They have a whole night safari at their zoo, so you can see the animals at night," Kara said.

"Sure," Callie said, before she suddenly squeezed Grant's hand hard.

"What do you do, Grant? Aside from stay out of the sun, of course." Kara nodded to the server as a plate of food was set before her.

Grant tried to remember the story Callie had come up with. "I'm an archaeologist, specialising in early colonial farming practices in the eighteenth and nineteenth centuries." Because if there was one thing he could talk about, it was farming as he'd known it.

Knut's forehead wrinkled. "Isn't that just…digging?"

"You mean the farming, or the archaeology?' Grant asked.

They all laughed.

"Well, yes, they both are, but there's a lot more to the archaeology than that. Digging's just the first part. Afterward, you need to analyse your findings, and compare them against written sources from the time period. You see…" Grant droned on, aware of the polite smiles and nods from both Knut and Kara that signified he was boring them just enough to ensure they wouldn't ask him any further questions.

Until Callie's fork clunked to the table, and he heard her voice in his head, as clearly as if she'd spoken them: "Distract me."

Barely pausing in the middle of a description of early colonial land clearing practices – complete with tiger snakes – Grant did what he'd always done when Dana asked him to distract her during a dull dinner discussion.

THIRTY

When Uncle Lucius entered the dining room, Callie had grabbed Grant's hand to get his attention. All he did was squeeze back reassuringly, so she'd done her best to sink down in her seat and be as invisible as possible, so he wouldn't see her.

Then Grant launched into a story about some of the early European colonists trying to clear Australian trees with flimsy English tools.

Callie half listened, for he wasn't a bad story teller, and this tale sounded like he'd actually been there, two hundred years ago. Which…might actually be possible. She wasn't sure how long gargoyles lived for. They were statues, after all, which could endure for centuries, so a couple hundred years might be nothing to Grant.

Oh, fuck. Uncle Lucius chose a table directly in front of Callie, over by the window. He only had to look over here and he'd see her, and…

She prayed to the goddess, to every damn deity in the universe, to distract her so she didn't look at him. Because she didn't want to look at him. She wanted to forget he existed, and focus solely on the man…gargoyle…whatever Grant was…by her side, and her cousins across the table.

As if in answer to her prayer, something warm slid through the slit in the side of her skirt, skimmed across her thigh, then wiggled its way into her knickers and between her legs.

Gently stroking, like she'd imagined Grant's fingers would, if…

Only both of his hands lay on the table. Well, until he lifted one and laid it on top of hers, squeezing gently. He gave a tiny nod, as he continued talking about trees that broke axes faster than they fell.

But Callie couldn't focus on his words any more. All her attention was occupied by his…wait, was that his tail?

Sticking out the back of his waistband, snaking out from under his shirt and beneath her skirt, stroking her most intimate…

She gave a little gasp as he found exactly the right spot, circling it.

A sensible woman would grab his tail right where it met his arse and give it a mighty yank, to let him know how inappropriate this was. A sensible woman would close her legs and shake her head and not allow this to continue.

Except that his tail felt better than any vibrator, and far more distracting, too.

So instead of doing something sensible, she

parted her thighs wider to give him better access.

And then she could think of nothing else but that gloriously sinful tail, stroking her to heights of pleasure she'd never believed possible.

She didn't care that she was in the middle of a restaurant, sitting with her cousins. All she cared about was how close she was to the first orgasm any man had ever given her. And how much she wanted it.

Until she looked up, and met the gaze of Uncle Lucius.

Her dinner rose up in her throat, threatening to make her throw up. Any desire she'd felt vanished.

Callie jumped to her feet. "I don't feel well," she blurted out, before she bolted back to her room.

THIRTY-ONE

Grant followed Callie up the stairs, his heart weighing heavier with every step he took. He knew Callie wasn't Dana, yet when she'd said the same words, he'd reacted so automatically, he hadn't stopped to think. He never should have…

Callie threw open the door and raced for the bathroom, where she fell to her knees beside the toilet bowl, peering into it as though she might divine her future in the small circle of water.

Grant closed the door, then locked it behind him.

"I'm sorry," he began. "I should never have done that. It was the first thing I thought of, when you asked me to distract you, so I didn't stop to think whether I should. I should have asked your permission before touching you, let alone so intimately, and for that I'm truly, sincerely sorry. If there's anything I can do to make it up to you…"

Callie twisted, so instead of looking down, she peered up at him instead.

"You? I'm not mad at you. I mean, I was surprised, because the last thing I expected was for you to fuck me with your tail in front of my family, but once I got over my shock, it was…it was…" She reddened. "I'm not angry at you. I'm angry at…my uncle was there, watching me, like he knew what you were doing under the table and I couldn't…couldn't take pleasure in it any more. Not with him there."

Grant snorted. "So what I should have done instead was pick him up and toss him out of the restaurant. Or off the nearest cliff." Then he'd never be able to look at Callie and remind her of his past crimes again.

"No, you can't do things like that. No matter how much I'd like you to, it's just not…something you do." Callie clambered to her feet, and laid a hand on Grant's arm. "Thank you for thinking it, though. It's nice to know I have a champion, someone who'd defend me even if we're not living in medieval times any more. It's kind of sweet, actually."

Grant had been called many things in his life, but never sweet. Yet from Callie, he would take it as the compliment she evidently intended it to be.

"I should go back down there and apologise to Kara and Knut. But if I see him again, I know I'll be sick. I can't face him. That look on his face, exactly the same as the way he looked at me when I was eight…"

Grant took her hands in his. "Look at me,

Callie. Just me. There's no one else here. Just us. And I want you to listen to me. You're a powerful witch. The most powerful I've ever met. You managed to summon me back from the dead with a spell you found in a book. You cheated death itself, Callie. No man's any match for you when you put your mind to it. Any sane man should tremble in his boots for fear of arousing your displeasure."

She managed a weak smile. "You're the only man here, and you're not trembling."

He could not lie to her. Nor did he want to. "That's because I have no intention of arousing your displeasure. Instead, I'd like to offer to finish what I started downstairs, and distract you so thoroughly, you'll have room for no one else in your dreams but me tonight."

She wet her lips, naked longing shining in her eyes. She wanted him. Perhaps even as much as Grant wanted her.

"I am your protector, Callie. I cannot hurt you. But I can give you a great deal of pleasure, if you wish it."

"With your…tail?"

"With any part of me you might desire. My hands. My mouth. My tail. My body is yours to command. Tell me what you want, and it's yours."

"I've never…no man has ever…" she began, her cheeks reddening.

"You're never taken a lover before?" Grant asked. "I will be gentle, I promise."

Callie shook her head. "Oh, it's not that. I've slept with men before. But not one of them has given me any pleasure. So when you offer a great deal of it, it's hard to believe. I mean, the only pleasure I've ever had was with…" She pressed her lips together and reddened even more.

Ah. He plucked the object from her mind and understood. "Your vibrator, if that's what you call the silver device you used the other night. Which is in that drawer, if I remember correctly…" He rummaged in the cabinet beside the bed, and drew out the device.

Her mouth dropped open. "You were watching me?"

He ducked his head. "I am your protector. When your heartbeat sped up and your breathing grew rapid, I feared you were having another nightmare, so I checked on you. Only to find you were not asleep and it wasn't fear that made your heart beat faster. Please forgive my intrusion, and let me make it up to you now."

"I…" She looked longingly at the device in his hands. YES, PLEASE, her mind screamed, though her lips didn't move.

Grant took her in his arms, moving in close to kiss her. Softly, softly, giving her every chance to refuse him, to back away or push him away, if he asked too much.

But her lips welcomed him, her tongue twining with his, as she let out a little moan of longing.

MORE.

He scooped Callie up and carried her to the bed. Then he tugged down her skirt and her undergarments, baring her to the waist. Beautiful. So incredibly beautiful, and soaking wet just for him.

"I have only one request, Callie, if you are willing," Grant said, stroking her silken folds with his finger. God, but he wanted to taste her.

"Anything," she said. "If you can make me come." It came out as a challenge. One he would gladly meet.

Grant grinned. "When I make you come, I want to hear you scream for joy. I want to hear my name on your lips."

THIRTY-TWO

Grant stripped off his shirt, his eyes never leaving hers, but he kept his pants on. When she looked askance at them, he just grinned. "Tonight is all about your pleasure."

Probably for the best, she decided. This was mad enough without bringing his monster cock into it.

And then he held up her vibrator, gleaming silver in the light from the bedside lamp, until he coiled his tail around it. Then he switched it on, toying with the settings for a moment before he found one he liked.

He threw himself on the bed beside her, propping himself up on the pillows. "Come here," he said, pulling her into his lap. Now that decidedly large bulge pressed against her back, but she forgot all about it as his tail snaked around her waist and slid between her thighs, still wrapped around the vibrator like a snake with its prey.

His tail had felt so hot inside her downstairs…

If she'd still been wearing underwear, she'd have soaked through them all over again.

He rested his chin on her shoulder, watching his tail just as avidly as she was, as he eased it inside her.

Oh, goddess…

The hum of the vibrator against her clit was all it took to send her soaring into bliss, she'd been so close before. But Grant didn't stop there.

No, he thrust his tail deep inside her, keeping up a steady rhythm as he stroked her, all the while rubbing the vibrator against her clit. She'd barely caught her breath from the first orgasm before the second one tore through her, and she couldn't help but scream his name, just like he wanted.

No man had ever given her an orgasm before, and Grant had already given her two. A sensible girl wouldn't be greedy. She'd quit while she was ahead.

But somewhere in between the first orgasm and the second, Callie had completely lost her mind.

"More," she demanded. "Please."

Grant kissed her neck. "I will give you everything you desire."

THIRTY-THREE

The feel of her delicate body in his arms, shuddering with ecstasy as he pleasured her with his tail and the small humming device she liked so much…if Grant hadn't been sure Callie was the perfect woman for him, he'd be triply certain of it now.

He'd almost decided to stop after the third orgasm, to let her rest, until he heard heavy footfalls on the stairs.

The odious uncle, he was sure of it.

He would not allow the man to spoil Callie's night any further. She'd commanded him to distract her, and he would do just that. He'd be so damn distracting, she wouldn't even notice if the man broke down her bedroom door.

Though he'd better not, for then Grant would have to disembowel him, because there was no way he'd let the man escape punishment, no matter what Callie said about how times had changed.

But right now, his focus was on Callie, and the spot deep inside her that he'd just found. When he rubbed it just right, she let out the sweetest little moan that he just had to hear again. Oh, maybe if he pressed the humming device to that spot, and used his fingers, too…

Callie let out a wordless cry, writhing against him.

SO CLOSE. PLEASE DON'T STOP. SO CLOSE…

He could almost feel it, like her body was his own. Like she was somehow magically sharing her pleasure with him along with her thoughts.

Heavy footsteps approached her door.

"Come for me, darling," Grant said loudly. "Come for me now."

"Yes…yes…YES!"

Her ecstasy overflowed into him, until Grant could scarcely breathe, but he kept up his furious pace. She would come again, and again, and again, focussed solely on him, so she didn't even notice her uncle had come to visit, until the man was long gone.

"Come for me, Callie. Let me hear you scream my name."

"Oh, Grant, I'm going to…I'm going to…"

"Again, darling. Come for me, again."

"Grant, oh, Grant…"

"Come for me now."

"Oh, yes, please, Grant, oh, goddess…GRANT!"

Anyone listening might have made the mistake of thinking Grant held all the power in Callie's bedroom that night, and while he certainly wasn't powerless, he knew the truth – that he was hopelessly, irrevocably bound to her, and he wouldn't have it any other way.

He would give her the world, or maybe even the whole universe, just to hear her scream his name like that again.

But he'd start with another bevy of orgasms, because he could not resist the enchantress in his arms.

THIRTY-FOUR

Her evil uncle had long since retired to his own bedroom by the time Grant was done with Callie, and she fell into an exhausted sleep. Grant's pants were uncomfortably tight, for he had maintained his insistence that tonight was all about her pleasure, and not her own. Though how it was possible for him to get harder than actual stone remained a mystery to him. Perhaps if he took himself in hand for just a moment, he might be able to relieve a little of the pressure…

Heavy footsteps approached the door again.

No. Grant would not allow the bastard to wake her. He slipped out into the passage, to meet the vile man before he could reach Callie's door.

"I came to ask Calliope to go fishing with me," the man said uncertainly.

Grant didn't believe a word of it. "Callie's quite worn out. She's sleeping now. But I'll come fishing with you. It's been a while since I've caught anything worth cooking. Tell me, is it true the fish on the coast here are big enough to feed a whole family?"

He knew it had been true two hundred years ago, for he and his cousins had eaten more fish stew than bread in their first year in the Swan River Colony.

The man puffed up his chest, as though the size of the fish were his doing. "Some of them are big enough to feed them for days. But you need to know how to catch them, and the best spots. I'll show you. Then maybe Calliope can come with me tomorrow."

Over Grant's dead body. Or not even then, for he wasn't sure whether having a body of living stone made him alive or dead, or something combination of both.

"Lead the way!" Grant said, and followed the man out of the hotel.

THIRTY-FIVE

Lucius's horseless carriage was much larger than Callie's, with more seats.

Before Grant could remark on the difference, Lucius said, "I coach the state girls' hockey team. Well, a couple of them, actually. Sometimes I give the girls a lift when we're travelling."

"They travel with you? Alone, with no chaperone?" Grant asked.

Lucius stared at him. "What lies has Calliope told you?"

Grant only grinned. "Callie has no secrets from me."

The man looked decidedly uncomfortable at that, fumbling with his keys for a long moment before he managed to open the door to the carriage. "Get in."

For a moment there, Grant had expected the man to revoke his invitation, but the open door said otherwise. Grant just shrugged and climbed into the carriage.

The bumpy ride down to the beach was more like Grant remembered the few carriage rides he'd taken in the past, though the road didn't look any worse than the ones Callie had travelled along. Perhaps Lucius's vehicle or driving skills were as inferior as the man himself, Grant decided.

They stopped in a parking place surrounded by rocks, with signs every few yards stating how dangerous the rocks, cliffs and waves were. "Are you sure this is a good place to catch fish?" Grant asked doubtfully. He'd pulled them in from the beach easily in the past, but the ocean currents might have changed in the last two centuries.

"Of course! You want to catch a big one, don't you?"

He certainly didn't want to catch something too small to eat, so Grant just nodded, took the fishing poles Lucius passed to him, and followed him out over the rocks to what Lucius insisted was the best spot.

The spot in question was a cliff perched over a churning maelstrom – definitely not somewhere Grant wished to drop his fishing hook. Why, the water would likely take off with his fishing pole and leave him with nothing.

Lucius evidently noticed Grant's doubt. "The trick is to cast your rod out over the rocks into the pool on the other side. That's where the big ones lurk." He pointed, then baited his hook and demonstrated. Sure enough, his line soared out over the rocks and landed in the calm water on the other side. "You try."

Grant's first cast fell short, landing on the rocks. He wound the line in to try again. A gust of wind caught his second try, plunging it into the whirlpool below. He leaned over the cliff as he tried to pull the line back up for a third try.

Only for Lucius to give him an almighty shove that sent him clean over the cliff, plummeting toward the foaming water below.

THIRTY-SIX

It only took Grant one panicked moment to remember he had wings, which easily tore through his shirt before sending him soaring back up to the cliff face to confront the man who'd tried to murder him.

The man who'd raped Callie countless times AND tried to murder him.

Grant's fury boiled over. Not trusting himself to speak, he simply snatched up the maggot and flew out to sea.

Lucius began to gibber and struggle.

Grant flew higher.

The man's struggling grew wilder, so that Grant had a hard time keeping a hold of the man. Maybe he'd scared him enough, and should head back to shore now.

Then Grant spotted a rock about a hundred yards from shore, isolated from the beach by a mess of foam, breaking waves and sharp rocks. Perhaps he'd set the man down there and leave him for a day to think on his actions, before coming back tomorrow night.

The more he thought about it, the more he liked this idea.

Grant veered to the side, searching for a flat place to drop the man. Ah, he found the perfect spot – on the far side of the rock from the beach, so no one would see him from shore.

Something wet splashed against him. Funny, the waves surely couldn't reach him this high.

He recoiled in disgust. It wasn't the waves at

all. The maggot had pissed himself.

Grant flapped faster. He couldn't reach the rock fast enough.

Only Lucius had other ideas. Still struggling wildly in his now soaking wet clothes, he was slipperier than an eel, and with one determined squirm, he managed to break free of Grant's grip, only to tumble, screaming, down to the rock below.

The screaming ended in a horrible crunch, then silence, where the only thing Grant could hear was the breaking of waves.

Blazes, what would Callie say?

THIRTY-SEVEN

Sunrise was approaching. Grant had time for a quick dip in the water, to wash off the foul stench of Callie's incontinent uncle, before he flew back to the hotel. Callie was still asleep when he slipped back into her room.

Maybe he didn't need to tell her. Her uncle had gone fishing and simply been washed off the dangerous cliffs he'd had no regard for. It wasn't like anyone had seen them together, or seen Grant himself there at all. Even if they had, who would believe that they'd seen a winged monster over the water? Even Grant himself would laugh at such a story.

Or he would have, if he didn't have wings.

Which Callie knew about, so she'd automatically suspect him.

But it didn't matter. No one had seen him. He was sure of it.

When Callie woke, she greeted him with a kiss and a soft thank you, along with a faint blush. Of course, one kiss was not enough, and she was soon breathless.

"Stop, stop! The wedding's tonight, and Kara will be worried after I ran off last night, so I have to go downstairs early to reassure her I'm all right. Then there's hair and makeup and photos, before the ceremony tonight. I have to shower, and go down to the restaurant for breakfast. Will you…will you come with me? In case Uncle Lucius is there?" Anxious eyes begged him.

"Of course I'll be there to protect you," he

said easily, then forced himself to add, "but I know your uncle went fishing early this morning, and I didn't hear him return." Nor would he, without some serious magic or maybe a necromancer. But of course Grant couldn't say that, or Callie would know he'd killed him.

That earned him another kiss, which he knew he didn't deserve. "Thank you!" Then she skipped into the bathroom and closed the door.

THIRTY-EIGHT

"Have you seen Uncle Lucius anywhere?" Kara asked the moment Callie stepped into the restaurant for breakfast. "He was supposed to pick up the flowers first thing this morning, and the florist just rang to say he hasn't arrived."

"He went fishing early this morning. Maybe he's forgotten," Grant offered.

"What's your Uncle Lucius done now?"

Aunt Cecelia marched into the room, looking harassed.

"He's forgotten to pick up the flowers, Mum! The florist called to say she has a delivery coming in this afternoon, and if we don't pick our order up before noon, she won't have space in the fridge for them. The hotel here has space in the cool room all ready, but someone needs to go pick them up. He had one thing to do, Mum, and he's managed to ruin that. I told you we never should have asked him."

"He's my little brother. Family. You couldn't do that," Kara's mother said.

Of course Aunt Cecelia was the one who'd insisted he get an invitation. But Callie's life would be a million times easier if she hadn't.

"Can you go?" Kara begged Callie.

Callie began to shake her head. No way was she going anywhere she might see Uncle Lucius. At least here she could run up to her room and lock the door.

"Callie can't go! She's first to see the

hairdresser. See how long her hair's gotten? It's going to take hours. I'll go," Aunt Cecelia said.

"Thanks, Mum."

Callie wasn't sure who was more relieved – Kara or her – as Aunt Cecelia trotted down the steps to the carpark.

"Now, I don't care what Mum says. You need breakfast before you have your hair done." Kara grabbed Callie's arm and began to tug her toward the breakfast buffet. "They bring in fresh bread from the bakery up the road every morning, and they'll do your eggs however you like them. C'mon, Grant, tell her she needs a good breakfast, especially after she didn't finish dinner last night. It's going to be a busy day."

Without Uncle Lucius there, Callie's heart felt a hundred times lighter. She allowed herself to be led to the trough…okay, the bain maries…so she could fill a plate for breakfast.

Kara chattered nonstop about the day's complicated schedule, which hadn't changed from the last time Callie had heard it, so she just nodded in between bites.

Then it was off to meet the hair stylist, who wanted to do something that involved curls and braids and enough hairpins to stab a hundred Caesars to death. Kara's eyes shone at whatever she and the stylist envisioned, so Callie just nodded and agreed to it all. Then she caught sight of a grinning Grant in the shadows behind her in the mirror, and whatever worries she'd had melted away.

Still riding the post orgasm high from last night. The multiple orgasm high, actually, though she'd lost count somewhere after the first three. Maybe tonight, when the wedding was over and they were alone in her room together, she'd let him use more than just his tail.

Yes. That's the thought she focussed on, every time Kara panicked or something didn't go exactly according to plan or someone mentioned Uncle Lucius. Who no one had seen since last night, apparently, to Callie's relief.

Maybe she'd be really lucky and he'd spend so long fishing, he forgot to turn up to the wedding at all.

Well, she could hope.

THIRTY-NINE

As the day progressed, Callie transformed from the terrified creature she'd been last night to the powerful, take-no-nonsense witch who'd summoned Grant to her side in the cemetery. He'd never watched a fine lady at her toilette before, but even then, he had to admit that the women who worked their mundane magic on Callie made her even more beautiful than he'd thought possible. He swore her dark eyes could read his soul, and all his secret desires.

Or make him spill all his secrets, for her alone.

Even her nails had intricate runes painted on each one, in a language Grant did not understand.

Finally, the sun set, and Callie headed up to her room to dress.

Grant hovered on the threshold, knowing she did not need him to guard her any more, because the threat to her was gone.

But still he couldn't bring himself to tell her.

Callie beckoned. "Come in. Someone has to stand watch while I get dressed. Besides, it's not like you haven't seen me naked already."

And he hoped to again, if she would permit him. Smothering a smile, Grant obeyed.

"Now, help me get this tied," she ordered, tugging a corset down over her torso.

Grant opened his mouth to ask her why she hadn't donned an underdress beneath it, like the ladies of his time had, then closed it again.

Women of this time weren't the same, or their clothes weren't, and he'd be a fool to do anything to delay touching her again when he wanted nothing more. So he laced up the corset, admiring the swell of her breasts as he tied the lacings, before helping her to pin her stockings in place.

He ached to take her now, just like this, but he didn't dare suggest it. She had a wedding to attend. Maybe afterwards, if he was very lucky, she'd allow him to pleasure her as he had last night. He didn't dare hope for more.

Not after he'd killed her kinsman.

Next came the gown, a confection made of multiple diaphanous layers that he feared would be too thin to cover her with any degree of modesty, but as the fabric settled over her curves, he was surprised to find he'd been wrong. Oh, some parts of the dress were still a little sheer, but they hinted at the shape underneath instead of showing her silhouette outright.

The top layer of cloth glittered silver in the

light, shimmering and catching the eye like she'd been clothed in pure starlight.

An enchantress indeed.

"How do I look?" she asked, turning slowly on the spot so the skirt flared out around her.

Grant opened his mouth, but no words came out. He cleared his throat and tried again. "Like a goddess. Like I should fall to my knees in worship and beg to be allowed to kiss your feet."

She laughed. "Tonight, when the wedding is over, and we come back up here, if you help me undress, I'll let you kiss me wherever you like."

He should tell her. She deserved to know.

But if he told her, there'd be no kissing. Not now, not ever.

"Now if only I can manage to avoid Uncle Lucius for the rest of the day, and not make a mess of Kara and Knut's wedding blessing, today will be absolutely perfect."

Grant wet his lips. She deserved to know. Just the knowledge that she never needed to be afraid of that wastrel ever again was worth a thousand kisses. No, a million.

"He won't be coming. You'll never see him again, Callie." Grant took a deep breath. "He can't come to the wedding because he's dead. I accidentally killed him last night."

She jerked back, out of his reach, horror in her eyes. "You killed my uncle?"

"Not on purpose. He tried to kill me, so I got angry, and I only meant to scare him, but then things got out of hand and he fell…" Grant swallowed. "He didn't survive the fall."

She looked almost afraid to ask. "What did you do with the body?"

"I left it there on the rock. It was almost dawn and I didn't have time to do anything except fly back here before the sun rose, because I knew you needed me here."

"What if someone finds it?"

"They won't. It's on a rock, a hundred yards out to sea, out of view from the shore, and there's nothing but shoals and white water surrounding it, so no boat can reach it."

"How did it get there?"

"I was flying over the rock with him and he fell."

"So only someone who can fly could find him?"

Grant smiled. "Yes."

Callie blew out an exasperated breath. "So every kitesurfer, skydiver and pilot in the southwest might see him. Not to mention anyone with a drone. It's only a matter of time."

"You mean…people can fly in your time?"

"Yes, of course they can. Not with wings, like you, but with machines and…you know what? I don't have time to discuss dead bodies with you right now. But this isn't over. As soon as we're done celebrating my cousin's wedding, you're going to take me out to that rock to see that body."

Grant bowed his head. "Yes, mistress."

"You know I hate it when you call me that!"

"Yes, Callie."

She shoved her feet into her shoes, and

marched out of the room, with Grant trailing after her.

Yes, he'd done the right thing in telling her.

But why did he think he'd made a terrible mistake?

FORTY

This was it. Kara and Knut had said their vows, and they stood with their hands joined, looking to Callie to finish the ceremony with the traditional Viking blessing. First she said it in Norse, proud that she didn't stumble over the words even once. If Uncle Lucius had been here, she might have, but Grant had taken care of that little problem for her.

Accidentally dropping him on a rock

offshore. Of all the ways she'd hoped karma would come for Lucius, that wasn't one she'd ever considered.

Everyone was still looking at her. Oh, right. She was supposed to say the blessing in English, too, so everyone understood.

Callie cleared her throat.

"From this day, there shall be but one end for you both, one bond after your vows, nor shall your first love aimlessly perish. Happy are you both to have won the joy of such a consort, for neither of you will descend in death to an underworld where you will be lonely. So let the encircling bonds grip both your throats…" She'd already handed them the traditional necklaces during the Norse version, and they wore them proudly now. "The final anguish shall bring you nothing but pleasure, and the certain hope of renewed love, for death shall grant you new delights. Each world holds joy, and in each realm in which you reside may the repose of your united souls win fame through your faithfulness and love."

Everyone clapped, and then it was time to sign the register, for Kara had insisted Callie be her witness.

Yet as Callie stood there, waiting for Kara and Knut to finish signing the paperwork, she couldn't help but think about the blessing she'd spoken. Vikings hadn't just thought about life, but death, and they feared death less because they had a companion who'd fight alongside them equally. Risking death for each other, killing anyone who threatened them.

Wasn't that what Grant had done? Okay, he had said he'd killed Uncle Lucius by accident, but he also said Lucius had tried to kill him first. Which kind of made it self defence. Sort of. Viking love was about having someone to kill for or die for. Both of which Grant had done for her with Uncle Lucius. Her living stone champion, like a medieval knight from the past come to save her in the present.

She could hardly stay angry at him for that. Not when she'd just wished the same thing for Kara and Knut.

The celebrant waited for Callie to put her signature on the papers, before adding her own. Then the celebrant said something about husband and wife, and Callie found herself following Kara and Knut through a tunnel of fairy lights back to the main house.

The dinner and the speeches went by in a blur. Dancing and cake were done, and it seemed almost no time at all before they were farewelling Kara and Knut, as the couple headed off to the bridal suite for a private celebration, just the two of them.

Whereas Grant had kept his distance, his sorrowful eyes watching Callie from the edge of the room. Until now.

All night, he'd never wavered once. Every moment, he'd protected her. Exactly what he'd sworn to do. She pulled off the dress and laid it across a chair, promising herself she'd put it away properly in the morning. She was too impatient to do any more except pull on some ordinary clothes more suitable for venturing out into the winter night.

"Right, let me grab my car keys and a torch, and let's go," Callie said.

Grant shook his head. "You won't need those. It'll be easier to fly."

FORTY-ONE

Grant waited until they were outside before he stripped off his shirt and spread his wings.

"Are you sure you can carry me?" Callie asked.

"You weigh half what your uncle did, and I could have carried him twice the distance without a problem. I only dropped him because he twisted out of my grip. I only meant to scare him because I was angry. I didn't think, and then he was struggling and we were in midair and he fell and by the time I swooped down to catch him, it was too late." Grant shook his head. It had all happened so fast. Too fast to make sense of it. The worst part was that he didn't regret it. Lucius had been a vile man who'd deserved to die, and the universe had obliged, with Grant's help. He only hoped Callie would forgive him for his part in it.

"All right," Callie said, holding out her arms. "What do I do?"

Grant wrapped his arms around her in a lover's embrace he wished with all his heart she'd allow him to know again. One day. But today, he would hold her tighter than ever before, because he would not let her go until her feet returned to the ground.

Then, with one mighty sweep of his wings, they were airborne, rising up, as Callie turned her face heavenward in the rushing wind.

"Oh, this is amazing," she breathed.

No struggling or screaming for his

wonderful witch. No, she was his fearless goddess as they flew higher.

All too soon, the land ended and the water began, swirling around the rocks Lucius had intended use to kill Grant, instead of himself. Then Lucius's bane, the rock bigger than the rest rose up, and Grant circled it, looking for the man's remains.

There!

Grant swooped down, scanning the rock for a spot to land, just as he had last night. Lucius's body was sprawled across half of it, but there was still enough space for the two of them, if they stood close. He didn't release Callie, though, even as he spun her around so that she might face the corpse that had been her tormentor.

Callie pulled something out of her pocket, and clicked it. The rock was flooded with light, and a hundred small crabs scurried out of its beam.

"They were eating him," she said. "Ugh, you can barely even see his face."

Sure enough, she was right. Crabs or sea birds or something else had already attacked the man. If Grant hadn't known it was Lucius, he wouldn't have recognised him.

"Wait…is that his heart?" she asked, edging closer.

Grant knew little of human anatomy, so he stayed silent.

Callie peered closer. "Yes, I think it is. Help me get it out."

Grant raised his hand and extended his claws, then used them to dig out the offending organ. "Here." He held it out, blood dripping from his fingers.

Callie scanned the rock, searching for something. "What we need is a bag or…oh, look, there's a bucket. Can you grab it? Put the heart in that."

Wedged in a crevice between two rocks was the bucket she'd spotted, and it came out easily enough, along with a length of rope tied to the handle. He dropped the heart in the bottom, then swished his bloodied hand in the water, until it came out clean. Only then did he return to Callie with his offering.

She grabbed the bucket handle, her eyes still on the corpse. "It doesn't look like he fell from the sky at all. More like…a wave washed him up on this rock after he fell in, and he crawled up here and died of exposure. I suppose by the time someone does find him, the crabs will have mutilated him even more. Am I a bad person that I don't feel the slightest bit sorry that he's dead?"

Grant shook his head. "He did terrible things to you, and he tried to kill me. That's reason enough not to mourn him. He might have had other victims, too. Girls who are now safe." He coughed. "May I ask why you wanted his heart?"

She took a deep breath. "This is going to sound crazy, but there's a spell I'd like to try. I have no idea if it will work, but the spell says I need the heart of my kinsman to cast it, and seeing as he doesn't need it any more…" Callie shrugged.

"Will you allow me to stand by you and watch when you cast this spell?" Grant asked.

Callie didn't hesitate. "Absolutely. I wouldn't dream of casting something so dangerous without my faithful stone protector standing by my side. But that's something for another day. Right now, I just want to go back to the hotel, and my bed." She looked up at him. "Can we fly back now? I'll carry the bucket."

FORTY-TWO

"Can you ever forgive me?"

Callie turned to find Grant's dark eyes fixed on her as she undressed.

"For what?" she asked.

"For killing your evil uncle."

She laughed. Maybe she shouldn't have, with a man dead and all, but she'd been carrying the weight of what he'd done to her for so long, she deserved a little release. Or maybe…

"If you can forgive me."

"What for?"

She took a deep breath. "For being so selfish last night, without even thinking about your pleasure when you gave me so much. For falling asleep and leaving you to fight alone, when my uncle threatened your life. For summoning you from what was possibly your well deserved, comfortable afterlife to come and protect me, and then getting angry at you when you did exactly what I'd asked you to. Well, not in so many words, but you did what you did to protect me. It's like that Viking blessing I said over Kara and Knut. When you have someone to kill for, or die for, to fight by your side until the end, when you meet again in the afterlife for a new adventure. I mean, I only said the words over them, but you actually did it. So in Viking terms, we're just as married as Kara and Knut."

She almost wished it were so. Then she and Grant would be in bed together, making love for the rest of the night instead of talking about the one man she'd do anything to forget.

"In Scotland, or at least the Scotland I remember, we're not married yet. The tradition there is to steal a bride, and the only vows you need say are to one another, before consummating the marriage. I always hoped I'd find a woman who'd be willing to let me steal her." Grant looked wistful.

Callie pulled off her sweater, then struggled out of her jeans. Goddess, she still had her stockings on underneath. "Where would you take me, if you were to steal me? Do you have some secret love nest, where you take all the women you want to seduce?" She took off her shirt, so all she wore was her corset, stockings and knickers.

Grant grinned. "Actually, I do have a place in mind. And a mind to steal you."

Before she could protest, he picked her up, threw her over his shoulder, and leaped out the window.

FORTY-THREE

"What is this place?"

They'd been flying for scarcely a moment before Grant set her on her feet again, so they couldn't have gone far.

"I saw it on my way in last night, and as there wasn't any light here tonight, I figured we might have it all to ourselves. I think it's a secret observatory, for looking at the stars."

"But it's so dark, I can't see anything!"

Then Grant flicked on the light switch, and she could.

The large telescope in the corner certainly gave her the same impression as Grant had gotten. With all the glass walls and windows, and nothing to obscure the view of the whole sky, this place would be perfect for stargazing.

Except…after last night, she'd really been hoping…

"This is where I confess I've never actually seduced a woman before. Like you, I've had lovers, though those were all a long time ago, and until tonight, I'd never found a woman I wanted to steal as a bride before. So I suspect I'm probably doing this arse-about, but…Callie, I've killed for you. I nearly died for you. I'll fight for you every day of my life, or yours, whichever is longer. I have wanted you since the moment I first saw you, and I want to spend every night giving you more pleasure than the night before. Starting tonight." He spread his arms wide. "Will you have me, Callie?"

While she'd been staring at the stars, he'd been stripping off, and now he sat on an enormous daybed, propped up against a mountain of pillows, with his monstrous cock pointing right at her.

This was what a good dick looked like, Tacey had said. That mythical kind of manhood that made sex worth having all night, and into the next morning.

But it was so BIG…

"Will it fit?" she asked, dropping to her knees on the bed beside him.

"Only one way to find out." He extended a claw, and sliced through her knickers, so they fell in ribbons of black lace onto the bed, leaving her bare. "Take me, Callie. Take all of me."

She couldn't resist him any longer. Callie climbed into his lap, straddling him so the tip of his cock pressed against her clit. Hot and hard and…

She sank down, moaning as he filled her until she could take no more, because she'd taken the whole length of him inside her.

"Put your hands on my shoulders," he whispered, as his hands circled her waist, tugging down her corset until her breasts popped free. "Now ride me. As hard as you like."

Only every time she drove down, he thrust up, in perfect synchrony, until she could no more stop than she could still her thrumming heart.

"Come for me, Callie," Grant commanded.

She was so close. So close. Yet she couldn't. Not yet.

He leaned forward and sucked on first one nipple, then the other, sending bolts of lightning right into her core. "Come for me, Callie," he growled.

Her eyes locked on his. "Not unless you come for me, Grant."

"Blazes, lass, I'm a gargoyle. Living stone. I can't…"

"Come for me, Grant," she commanded, clenching down hard on him as she felt the orgasm building. She could not resist for much longer.

A moment. An instant. No more.

Grant let out a roar the same time as she screamed his name, letting the waves wash over her for what felt like the longest orgasm of her life.

She'd scarcely caught her breath from the first one before she felt Grant move beneath her. "Another!" he growled, thrusting deep.

Another and another and another again…

FORTY-FOUR

Before dawn, Callie staggered down the steps to her car, finally understanding why Rochelle had struggled so much with the stairs at the Shut Up Café after she'd had a night of hot sex.

If a man who gave good dick was a unicorn, then Grant the gargoyle was the monster king of absolutely amazing dick. Goddess, and she'd thought that night he pleasured her with his tail had been good.

Her knickers were soaked just thinking about last night. Damn it, she had to drive.

"Right, I have the box of ice you wanted," Grant said, handing her the cooler before slipping under the blanket on the back seat.

The cooler of ice that now held Uncle Lucius's frozen, vacuum packed heart. Callie tucked it behind the passenger seat, before tossing another blanket over it to keep it insulated for the ride home.

She'd come a long way from the day she'd unearthed that spell book in her box of old school things. Just like her eight year old self, before Uncle Lucius, she now knew without a doubt that magic and monsters existed.

But now she knew she had the power to wield that magic, and command the monsters. And with Grant by her side, and the heart of her kinsman to fuel the spell, next time she summoned a demon, she'd get a real one this time, and no one would ever hurt her again.

Or so she thought…

ABOUT THE AUTHOR

Demelza Carlton has always loved the ocean, but on her first snorkelling trip she found she was afraid of fish.

She has since swum with sea lions, sharks and sea cucumbers and stood on spray drenched cliffs over a seething sea as a seven-metre cyclonic swell surged in, shattering a shipwreck below.

Demelza now lives in Perth, Western Australia, the shark attack capital of the world.

The *Ocean's Gift* series was her first foray into fiction, followed by her suspense thriller *Nightmares* trilogy. She swears the *Mel Goes to Hell* series ambushed her on a crowded train and wouldn't leave her alone.

Want to know more? You can follow Demelza on Facebook, Twitter, YouTube or her website, Demelza Carlton's Place at:

www.demelzacarlton.com

More Books by Demelza Carlton

<u>Colony: Holiday series</u>

Cowboys and Aliens (#1)

Ghost (#2)

Vulcan (#3)

Cupid (#4)

Valentine(#5)

Prometheus (#6)

<u>**Colony: Aqua series**</u>

Halcyon (#1)

Poseidon (#2)

Apollo (#3)

<u>**Colony: Nyx series**</u>

Fang (#1)

Talon (#2)

Claw (#3)

<u>Siren of Secrets series</u>

Ocean's Secret (#1)

Ocean's Gift (#2)

Ocean's Infiltrator (#3)

<u>**Siren of War series**</u>

Ocean's Justice (#1)

Ocean's Widow (#2)

Ocean's Bride (#3)

Ocean's Rise (#4)

Ocean's War (#5)

How To Catch Crabs

<u>**Nightmares Trilogy**</u>

Nightmares of Caitlin Lockyer (#1)

Necessary Evil of Nathan Miller (#2)

Afterlife of Alana Miller (#3)

Romance a Medieval Fairytale series

Enchant: Beauty and the Beast Retold

Dance: Cinderella Retold

Fly: Goose Girl Retold

Revel: Twelve Dancing Princesses Retold

Silence: Little Mermaid Retold

Awaken: Sleeping Beauty Retold

Embellish: Brave Little Tailor Retold

Appease: Princess and the Pea Retold

Blow: Three Little Pigs Retold

Return: Hansel and Gretel Retold

Wish: Aladdin Retold

Melt: Snow Queen Retold

Spin: Rumpelstiltskin Retold

Kiss: Frog Prince Retold

Reflect: Snow White Retold

Roar: Goldilocks Retold

Cobble: Elves and the Shoemaker Retold

Float: Enchanted Horse Retold

Steal: Forty Thieves Retold

Call: Pied Piper Retold

Fall: Scheherazade Retold

Feather: Swan Maidens Retold

Cross: Billy Goats Gruff Retold

Weave: Rapunzel Retold

Claim: Puss in Boots Retold

Curse: Rose Red Retold

Cross: Three Billy Goats Gruff Retold

Weave: Rapunzel Retold

Claim: Puss in Boots Retold

<u>**Heart of Stone series**</u>

Heart of Steel (#0)

Broken Chains (#1)

Broken Bonds (#2)

Broken Dreams (#3)

<u>**Heart of Steel series**</u>

Heart of Steel (#0)

Stone Guardian (#1)

Stone Champion (#2)

Stone Sentinel (#3)

Stone Shadow (#4)